Gwyneth Rees is half Welsh and half English and grew up in Scotland. She went to Glasgow University and qualified as a doctor in 1990. She is a child and adolescent psychiatrist, but has now stopped practising so that she can write full-time. She is the author of *Mermaid Magic*, *Fairy Dust*, *Fairy Treasure*, *Fairy Dreams*, *Fairy Gold*, *Cosmo and the Magic Sneeze* and, for older readers, *The Mum Hunt*, *The Mum Detective*, *The Mum Surprise*, *My Mum's from Planet Pluto* and *The Making of May*. She lives in London with her two cats.

The Mum Hunt won the Younger Novel Category of the Red House Children's Book Award 2004.

Visit www.gwynethrees.com

D0954414

Gwyneth Rees

Cosmo
and the
Great Witch
Escape

Illustrated by Samuel Hearn

MACMILLAN CHILDREN'S BOOKS

First published 2006 by Macmillan Children's Books
a division of Macmillan Publishers Limited
20 New Wharf Road, London N1 9RR
Basingstoke and Oxford
www.panmacmillan.com

Associated companies throughout the world

ISBN-13: 978-0-330-43733-2
ISBN-10: 0-330-43733-X

3 5 7 9 8 6 4 2

A CIP catalogue record for this book is available from
the British Library.

Typeset by Intype Libra Ltd
Printed and bound in Great Britain by Mackays of Chatham plc, Kent

For Ethan and Wilf

And with thanks to Oscar Shaw
for his feline input

1

Cosmo's mother, India, had just finished washing him very thoroughly with her rough pink tongue, and now she took him to have a look at himself in the mirror.

'See how clean and shiny your ears are now,' she told her kitten proudly, as they looked into the glass together. 'And your white bits are spotless too. You really must try harder to keep them that way, Cosmo.'

'Yes, Mother,' Cosmo mewed. Thankfully he was mostly black in colour like his father, but he had inherited his white paws and the white tip on the end of his tail from his mother – and those were the parts that he found most difficult to keep clean whenever he went outside to play.

India was an elegant, white short-haired

cat with emerald-green eyes, whose great-great-great-grandmother had been a cat of a very high pedigree flown to this country from India when her human family had moved here. Cosmo loved to hear his mother's stories about the beautiful, faraway country she had been named after, where apparently all the mice were curry-flavoured.

'I think you would look beautiful in a sari, Mother,' Cosmo told her now, as he watched her wrap herself up in a very fine gold-and-red shawl that had been draped over the back of a bedroom chair.

Cosmo's father, Mephisto, came into the room then, and India quickly extracted herself and went over to inspect *his* ears. India saw the cleanliness of Mephisto's ears as her responsibility too, since he couldn't reach them himself, and today she thought they were looking a bit dirty. Mephisto was a cat

2

of high standing in the local community, which meant it was very important that he had clean ears at all times, so she set to work immediately.

Cosmo's father was a handsome jet-black cat with dark green eyes and very large paws and Cosmo wanted to grow up to be just like him. Unlike ordinary cats, Mephisto was a witch-cat, which meant he had special magic powers and could help witches with their spells. In particular, witch-cats were known for their powerful magic sneezes. A few weeks earlier, when Cosmo had reached the age of six months, he'd had to undergo a special test to see if he was a witch-cat like his father or an ordinary cat like his mother. To his delight he had turned out to be a witch-cat, which meant he was able to assist witches with their spells, ride broomsticks and do all sorts of other exciting magical things.

Until recently, Cosmo's family had lived in the garage rather than the house, because the witch who had lived there had been a very nasty one called Sybil, who had ended up being sent to Witch Prison after brewing up a particularly evil spell. Even thinking about Sybil made Cosmo shiver, though his parents had reassured him that she could no longer harm him. Bad witches were only ever allowed out of prison to do community service – being made to help others was the one punishment every bad witch dreaded – and at those times they were securely tagged with an electronic device which meant that they got turned into frogs if they tried to run away.

After Sybil had been sent to prison, a family of good witches had moved into her house instead. They were called the Two-Shoes family and they consisted of a very kind witch called Goody, her witch-husband, Gabriel, and their witch-daughter, Scarlett, who had quickly become Cosmo's

5

best two-legged friend. (Cosmo's best *four*-legged friend was a tabby kitten called Mia, who lived in the house next door.)

Today was a very special day for the Two-Shoes family, because early that morning Goody had gone into the local witch hospital to have a baby. Cosmo was pleased that Scarlett was going to have a new baby brother or sister, but he was also a bit worried that she wouldn't want to play with him as much when she wasn't an only child any more. Not that he was going to be an only kitten for very much longer either. India's tummy had been getting a lot bigger over the last few weeks and recently she had told him that she was expecting a new litter of kittens. Cosmo had been her first kitten – an only one, which was unusual since mother cats generally gave birth to several babies at once.

The cat flap sounded and Mephisto's ears instantly pricked up. Even though they were upstairs he had excellent hearing and could always tell if they had an intruder.

'It's probably just Felina,' India said. 'She's coming to examine me today.'

Felina was the local cat professor and she was also Mia's mother. The two of them lived next door with a very devoted and well-trained human called Amy. Felina was the cleverest cat in the neighbourhood, and other cats came from miles around to seek her advice and attend her lectures. Felina specialized in Humanology (the study of human behaviour) and she was also becoming an expert in the study of non-cat languages. Whereas all cats could understand spoken Human, Felina had taught herself to *read* it as well. And whereas most cats understood a bit of mouse language and dog language (which was one of the easiest languages to learn because it was so basic), Felina could also understand rabbit, hedgehog, bat, fox and several bird and fish dialects.

The day before, Felina had told India that by examining her tummy, she would be able to tell her exactly how many kittens were inside. She had studied the way humans did this and said that she saw no reason why a cat shouldn't be able to do the same. India couldn't imagine how Felina was going to do such a thing, but she had willingly invited her to try.

Felina arrived at the top of the staircase now, holding something very strange in her mouth. It seemed to be some sort of long grey rubber tube, which she was dragging along the ground behind her. At one end of the tube was a round flat metal object and at the other end there were two shorter tubes, each of which had a hard plastic knob on the end of it. When Cosmo went to sniff the plastic knobs, he found that they had wax on them.

'Be careful,' Felina mewed at him as she let go of the object. 'That's human earwax – it's not as clean as ours.'

'What *is* this thing?' India gasped, coming forward to tap the rubber tube with her paw very tentatively.

'It's called a stethoscope,' Felina informed them. 'I slipped in through the window of the doctor's surgery down the road and borrowed it. Human doctors use them to listen to heartbeats and I remember seeing a similar one last time Amy took me to the vet. I'm going to use it to tell you how many kittens you're going to have. Each kitten will have its own heartbeat so all I have to do is

9

put this stethoscope on your tummy, India, and count how many there are.'

'Oh, Felina, however do you know these things?' India said, amazed.

Even Mephisto, who tended not to be easily impressed by the skills of other cats, was clearly full of admiration for the cat professor's expertise as she carefully positioned her head in between the two plastic earknobs and picked up the end of the long grey tube between her teeth – clasping it near the round metal part which she plonked down on to India's swollen tummy.

India was purring loudly with excitement and Felina ordered her to stop because she couldn't hear properly. Felina slowly slid the metal part of the stethoscope over India's belly until she had covered the whole area. Then she shook her head to rid herself of the bits that were stuck in her ears and

started to look very pleased with herself. 'Nine kittens,' she announced.

'Nine!' India looked delighted.

'Are you sure there are that many?' Mephisto sounded alarmed.

Felina nodded. 'A very fine litter.'

'I shall have to start looking for a nice warm nesting place,' India said.

'A nice *large* nesting place, you mean,' Mephisto grunted.

'If there are nine of them, it's going to take you a long time to wash them all, isn't it, Mother?' Cosmo murmured. 'You probably won't have time to wash *me* as well!' And he suddenly felt quite welcoming towards the new arrivals.

Just then the telephone started ringing.

'That might be Scarlett,' Cosmo mewed excitedly. 'She said she'd ring as soon as there was any news.'

'I'd better go and listen to it,' Mephisto said, leading the way downstairs to where the phone and answering machine sat on the table in the hall. Cosmo followed him and they waited patiently for the ringing to stop and the recorded message to play, and then for the sound of the voice of the caller to come out of the answering machine.

'Hi, Cosmo! Hi, Mephisto and India! Are you there? It's Scarlett!' a girl's voice sang out. 'Mum's just had a baby boy. He's really cute and we're going to call him Spike. Mum's got her own room in the hospital so you can all come and visit him if you like. If you come on the broomstick you can fly right up to the window and land on the ledge. Mum's room is the third window from the right on the top floor. Dad and I are here and so is Aunt Bunty. See you later!'

'Let's go *now*, Father!' Cosmo miaowed. Cosmo was very good at broomstick-riding although he sometimes got a little bit broom-sick if they went too fast.

As Mephisto grunted something in reply, Cosmo rushed upstairs to tell India and Felina the good news.

Both of them were very excited too. 'I think I'm a little heavy to go broomstick riding now,' India said. (Although India wasn't a witch-cat, Mephisto had often

13

taken her for rides by hooking a basket on to the end of the broomstick for her to sit in.) 'But your father can go with you to the hospital.'

'Oh, *I* shan't go,' Mephisto said, yawning, as he followed Cosmo into the room. 'Babies don't interest *me* that much.' As India gave a little growl he hastily added, 'Of course, *kittens* interest me a great deal, my dear.' And he went over to give India's tummy a lick.

'Why don't you take Mia with you to the hospital, Cosmo?' Felina suggested. 'I'm sure she would love to see this new witch-baby. It will be very educational for her too. I was giving her a lesson on the newborns of other species only last week.'

'I'll go and ask her right now!' Cosmo said, zooming off down the stairs towards the cat flap.

Outside he looked up sharply as a broom-stick whooshed overhead with a witch on board he didn't recognize. Her long green cloak was flapping out behind her and she had a green pointed hat on her head – which meant she must be a witch-midwife. She looked like she was in a hurry, so perhaps she was on her way to deliver a witch-baby.

Cosmo remembered what his mother had told him about witch-midwives. 'A midwife is a special type of nurse who helps deliver babies. Witch-midwives have special uni-forms, which is how you can tell them apart from other witches – they always wear green pointy hats and green cloaks and they always carry a bar of green soap in their pocket. You see, it's very important for witches to have clean hands before they touch a newborn witch-baby, just like cats must have clean tongues before they lick a newborn kitten.'

15

Suddenly a gust of wind caught the broomstick and the witch-midwife tipped to one side. She didn't fall off her broom, but Cosmo saw that something had dropped out of her pocket. She had flown on before there was time to call out to her, so Cosmo jumped over the fence into the next garden to see if he could find whatever it was. It was probably just a bar of soap, he thought.

It took Cosmo a while to find the object, which was lying in one of the flower beds. It was a plastic bag with something green inside it that clearly wasn't soap. He picked up the bag with his teeth and dragged it out on to the lawn to inspect the contents more closely. To his amazement he saw that the bag contained green toenail clippings. All witches had green toenails – and toenail clippings were sometimes used as ingredients in witches' spells – but these were the

curliest, brightest-green toenails that Cosmo had ever seen. And most amazingly of all, they actually seemed to be *glowing*!

2

The Witch Hospital – a building that was very large and had no less than ten pink chimneys coming out of its roof – was disguised from human eyes by having a frontage that looked like an ordinary house and a sign on the gate that was invisible to humans. The top floor was the maternity unit, where witch-mothers gave birth to witch-babies, and it was staffed entirely by witch-midwives.

That afternoon Scarlett Two-Shoes was holding her newborn baby brother in her arms while her mother looked on from her bed. Scarlett's father had just gone with Goody's sister, Bunty, to fetch some cups of eye-of-newt tea from the hospital canteen.

19

'He's so cute,' Scarlett kept saying, over and over.

'He looks just like you did when you were a baby,' her mother told her, 'except that you had even curlier toenails.'

Scarlett unwrapped the blanket to have another look at baby Spike's green curly toenails, which were visibly glowing. 'Our

toenails don't glow like that, do they, Mum?' she said. 'So why do Spike's?'

'All witch-babies have glowing toenails,' her mother explained. 'It lasts for the first two weeks after they're born as a sort of protection against evil spells or illness. Once they've stopped glowing we'll trim them in the same way we trim our own toenails – but we mustn't cut them until then.'

'Some witches *don't* trim their toenails, do they, Mum?' Scarlett pointed out.

'Some witches prefer not to,' Goody agreed. 'They just wear very pointy shoes instead. But I find long toenails a bit of a nuisance myself.'

Just then a witch-midwife came into the room.

'Hello,' Goody greeted her. 'You're a new face.'

'I just came on duty,' the midwife said,

21

smiling to reveal a large gap in her top front teeth. 'I need to take your baby away to weigh him now. It won't take long.' She held out her arms for Scarlett to hand over Spike.

'He only got weighed this morning,' Goody said.

'Yes, we've had a problem with the scales I'm afraid. We're having to reweigh all the babies. Don't worry. It won't take long.'

Cosmo and Mia were riding Cosmo's broomstick towards the hospital, and Mia (who was riding in the broomstick's basket) was telling Cosmo everything she had learned from her mother about witch-babies. 'They're almost the same in appearance as human babies, but they're easier to look after. You never have to guess what's wrong with them if they start crying, you see. Their *left* ear always goes green if they've got a wet nappy, their *right* ear goes green if it's a dirty nappy, and their *nose* goes green if they need feeding.'

'That's really cool,' Cosmo said.

'I know. They have green belly buttons and green finger and toenails like all witches of course, but unlike adult witches their toenails are really curly.'

'*How* curly?' Cosmo asked as he steered the broomstick out of the way of a large mother blackbird who was too busy concentrating on keeping hold of the worm in her mouth to look where she was going. He was thinking back to the curly toenail clippings the witch-midwife had dropped. He had told Mia about finding them and how, in the end, he had left them in the garden, just in case the midwife realized she had lost them and came back to look for them.

'I don't really know – but the other thing

23

Mother told me
about witch-babies,'
Mia suddenly
remembered,
'is that they
have *magic* in
their toenails.'

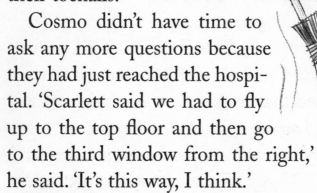

Cosmo didn't have time to
ask any more questions because
they had just reached the hospital. 'Scarlett said we had to fly
up to the top floor and then go
to the third window from the right,'
he said. 'It's this way, I think.'

'There's Scarlett!' Mia mewed a few
minutes later, and Cosmo brought the broomstick to such an abrupt stop that Mia nearly
fell out of the basket. They were directly
outside the window of Goody's room now.

Scarlett saw them and rushed to the

window to open it just as Bunty and Gabriel came back with four steaming cups of eye-of-newt tea (which was well known for having a soothing effect on witches, though unfortunately it tended to have a more allergic effect on humans). 'Cosmo! Mia! I can't wait to show you my baby brother. He's really cute,' Scarlett gushed.

'Where *is* Spike?' Gabriel asked, seeing that he was no longer in his cot, and Goody explained that he had just been taken to get weighed again.

'They've got catnip tea in the canteen,' Bunty told the kittens. 'But I expect you'd prefer a saucer of milk, wouldn't you?' She started to undo one of the little plastic pots of long-life milk which had come with the tea.

Mia mewed softly to Cosmo, 'That stuff tastes horrible. Amy gave it to us once –

25

before Mother trained her to only serve us the fresh kind.'

'It's OK – we're not thirsty,' Cosmo miaowed to Bunty, because Scarlett's aunt was one of the few witches who actually understood cat language.

'That sounds like Spike,' Goody suddenly said as a baby's cries became audible from outside their door. 'Gabriel, can you go and see?'

They could all hear the baby crying now, and as Gabriel opened the door, he almost tripped over a little white bundle that was lying on the floor. The bundle immediately started to bawl even louder and Gabriel quickly picked it up and brought it into the room.

'It's Spike,' he said. 'At least I *think* it is.' He was peering at the baby's face as if to make absolutely sure.

26

'Oh, how *could* they just leave him on the floor like that?' Goody sounded very upset, and her husband quickly put the wailing baby into her outstretched arms.

'One of my friends at school has a mum who's a nurse in a hospital,' Scarlett put in helpfully, 'and she says they're very short-staffed.'

'That's no excuse,' Goody snapped. 'Gabriel, go and fetch somebody! I'm going to make a complaint about this!'

Gabriel went away and came back a few minutes later with the head midwife. She was totally perplexed when Goody explained what had happened.

'There's nothing wrong with our weighing scales,' she said. 'Which midwife did you say it was who took him?'

'I'd never seen her before,' Goody replied. 'She said she'd only just come on duty.'

27

At that moment Cosmo and Mia heard raised voices coming from further up the corridor.

'Come on,' Mia said to Cosmo. 'Let's go and see what's happening.'

So Cosmo and Mia slipped out into the corridor and headed towards a room at the far end, where another witch-mother was clearly very angry about something. The two kittens went right into the room, where the distraught mother was telling a worried-looking midwife that her baby girl had just been taken off to be weighed – and been returned with all her toenails clipped off. She was showing the midwife the baby's feet, and Cosmo and Mia jumped up on to an empty chair to get a closer look. Instead of the long, curly glowing toenails that should have been there, all that was left were some short, straight green stumps.

28

The kittens raced back to Goody's room, where the witch family were still engaged in a heated conversation with the head midwife.

Cosmo leaped straight up on to the bed. 'Check Spike's toenails!' he mewed. 'Quickly!' When nobody seemed to take any notice of him he grabbed the end of Spike's blanket in his teeth and tugged the covers right off the baby's feet.

And then they saw that Spike's beautiful curly green toenails were gone. They had been trimmed right back.

After that everything happened in a whirl.

'That midwife must have been an imposter!'

'Oh, I never should have given Spike to her!'

'It's not your fault,' Gabriel tried to soothe his wife. 'How were *you* to know?'

As the head midwife rushed off to raise the alarm and the other midwives rushed from room to room, checking on the rest of the babies, Cosmo and Mia jumped back on to the window ledge to see if they could spot any suspicious broomstick traffic outside. 'I wonder if that midwife who stole Spike's toenails was the same one I saw flying over our garden,' Cosmo said to Mia. 'Maybe the toenails she dropped were ones that she'd already stolen.'

'You should tell the others about her,' Mia said. 'It might be important.'

So Cosmo tried to interrupt the witches' conversation, but found that it was very difficult to make himself heard. Finally Scarlett realized that Cosmo had something important to tell them, and she persuaded her family to be quiet so that he could speak.

'This is very worrying,' Bunty said after she had translated Cosmo's story for the others. 'I think I'd better go and report everything that's happened to the Good Witches' Society. Witch-babies' toenails contain a lot of magic. It's protective magic – that's what makes the toenails glow like they do – but if that magic gets into the wrong hands . . .' She shuddered.

'Will Spike be all right?' Scarlett suddenly asked. 'Doesn't he *need* his toenails to protect him?'

31

Before anyone could answer, the head midwife came back into their room and announced that all visitors must leave at once and that all the babies must now be kept in hospital under strict observation for at least the next few days. Their mothers were of course expected to stay in hospital with them. 'We don't know how this is going to affect the babies,' she added gravely. 'But they will definitely be more vulnerable to bad spells and nasty germs without their toenails.'

'I think the fathers had better stay too,' Gabriel said. 'I intend to be here if the witch who did this comes back again.'

'Scarlett had better come home with me then,' Bunty said. 'And Cosmo, I want you to go home too and tell Mephisto what's been happening. All witch-cats must be informed about this immediately.'

*

Cosmo and Mia rode home at top speed and when they got there Cosmo landed his broomstick in the garden where he had left the bag of toenails earlier. He wanted to take them to show to his father but, when he reached the flower bed where he had left them, he found that they were gone.

'That witch who dropped them must have come back for them,' Mia mewed. 'Unless . . .' She started to sniff around the flower bed just to make sure there was no unpleasant smell present, which might indicate that a dog had been there recently. Dogs were known for eating anything they came across – even toenails – because they didn't have such highly refined taste buds as cats.

'I wonder *why* the toenails were stolen?' Mia said, when she had satisfied herself that no dogs had visited this part of the garden recently.

'So they can be used as spell ingredients, probably,' Cosmo said.

'What sort of spells have witch-babies' toenails in them?' Mia asked.

'Very powerful ones, I guess,' Cosmo replied. 'But come on. Let's go and ask Father.'

3

When Cosmo and Mia burst in through the cat flap, they found that the kitchen was full of visitors. It looked as if Cosmo's parents were entertaining several of the neighbourhood cats. As well as Mia's mother, Professor Felina, there was a Siamese witch-cat called Tani, and her two Siamese kittens, Hagnus and Matty. Cosmo and Mia had first met Tani when she had rescued Mia from the jaws of a huge dog whose kennel they had got a bit too close to when they were younger kittens. Since then Cosmo's family had got to know Tani's family, and Cosmo and Mia had become friends with Hagnus and Matty, who were also witch-cats. There was another adult cat in the kitchen, who Cosmo didn't recognize. He

was a scruffy-looking short-haired grey with one blue eye and one green eye – and he had a very loud miaow.

Cosmo was used to the loud voices of his Siamese friends – his mother had told him that all Siamese cats spoke like that – but he was very surprised to hear such a loud voice coming from a cat who looked like he ought to have a perfectly ordinary miaow.

Hagnus and his sister came charging towards Cosmo and Mia, very excited to see them. Hagnus playfully grabbed Cosmo by the scruff and knocked him over and while the two boy kittens were tumbling around, Mia asked Matty who the strange grey cat was.

'That's Meowface Smith,' Matty explained. 'He's a quarter Siamese, which is why he's got such a loud miaow. His grandfather was Mother's great-uncle or something. He's a

37

travelling cat – and guess who he's been travelling with for the past six months?'

'How should I know?' Mia replied.

Matty took a deep, important-looking breath and announced, 'Meowface has been travelling with Cleo Cattrap.'

Mia stared at her. '*The* Cleo Cattrap?'

'That's right,' Matty said proudly.

Cosmo had overheard and now he stopped play-fighting with Hagnus in order to listen better.

Cleo Cattrap was one of the most famous cats in the country, chiefly because he had set up a travelling catwalk show, which he had named after himself. *Cleo Cattrap's Amazing Catwalk Extravaganza* drew in crowds of cats from far and wide whenever it came to town. So many cats wanted to enter the catwalk competition that Cleo was now having to hold auditions in each town he visited, where he invited cats to compete for the title of catwalk king or queen.

'Cleo wants to set up one of his catwalk competitions *here*, and Meowface is his chief assistant. They're looking for somewhere to hold the competition, so Meowface came to ask Mother if she knew of anywhere. It's got to be somewhere with quite a lot of space, where we won't be disturbed by any humans or witches.'

Cosmo and Mia were so excited they forgot all about the toenail robbery as they listened to the discussion that was taking place among the adult cats.

'If only I wasn't expecting nine kittens,' India said, 'I could have entered the competition myself.'

'India *is* one of the most elegant cats in the neighbourhood,' Mephisto told Meowface proudly. 'In fact, we are very well

39

matched. However, I would never enter a beauty contest myself. I think it would be most undignified.'

'This isn't just a beauty contest,' Meowface told him. 'Cats are also judged on deportment and vocal ability.'

'What does that mean?' Cosmo whispered.

'It means they're judged on how well they walk and talk,' Mia whispered back excitedly. 'Oh – this is so exciting! I wonder if kittens can enter!'

Unfortunately her mother, the professor-cat, overheard her. 'I would not wish you to waste your time on any competition that did not test your *brain* ability, Mia,' she mewed. 'Does this competition do that as well?' she asked Meowface.

'Well . . .' Meowface looked a little uncertain about that. 'All I can tell you is that Cleo

Cattrap is looking for what we in the business call the F factor.'

'The *F* factor?' The other cats looked none the wiser.

'The *Feline* factor,' Meowface explained grandly.

The professor-cat looked at him as if she thought he was incredibly stupid. '*Feline* means catlike,' she told him. 'And *all* cats are catlike, so what are you talking about?'

Meowface looked confused himself then. 'Cleo Cattrap will explain everything when he arrives,' he miaowed back quickly. 'In the meantime, has anyone got any ideas about where we could hold the competition?'

'How about in our garage?' India suggested.

'It's not big enough,' Meowface replied. 'We usually get a huge audience of spectator cats on the day. We need some sort of

41

human-sized hall, but a hall that isn't actually in human *use*, if you see what I mean.'

'What about Scarlett's school hall?' Cosmo said. Scarlett, like most other witch-children, attended the local human school (as well as having special Saturday morning witch lessons from a witch-tutor as well). 'It's the school holidays at the moment so the school will be shut and there won't be any humans there.'

'Brilliant!' Meowface said, grinning at him like a Cheshire cat instead of a quarter-Siamese one. 'Let's go and take a look at it.'

Just then the telephone started ringing.

Mephisto went to listen to the message while the others continued talking, and when he came back a few minutes later he told them they must turn on the television immediately.

'Why?' India asked.

'That was Scarlett. She says there's something very important on the local *Witch News*.'

Cosmo put his paw to his mouth in alarm as he remembered that he still hadn't told anyone about the incident at the hospital. 'Father, there's something I was meant to tell you,' he began, as all the cats trooped through to the front room, where Mephisto knocked the TV remote control on to the floor and trod all over it until he managed to switch it to the correct channel.

The *Witch News*'s reporter was looking very serious.

'Reports are coming in from all over the region that newborn babies' toenails are being stolen by witches posing as midwives. These fake midwives are entering hospitals and private homes and secretly clipping off the babies' toenails. All

parents of newborn witch-babies in the area are advised to be very wary in the wake of these extraordinary reports . . .'

'Father, that's what I was meant to tell you,' Cosmo mewed anxiously. 'Spike's toenails have been stolen and Bunty says that all witch-cats have to be on the alert!'

The two adult witch-cats in the room – Mephisto and Tani – looked very alert indeed as they heard this.

'I lived with a human once who used nail-clippers to clip my claws,' Meowface told them. 'I didn't like it because it stopped me scratching the stair carpet properly – but I didn't report my claws as *stolen*. Do you think I ought to have done?' He flexed his claws in a teasing sort of way at the kittens.

'Be quiet, Meowface,' Mephisto snapped. 'This isn't something to joke about. Witch-baby toenails have a lot of magic in them – they are one of the most powerful of all spell ingredients. Since you aren't a witch-cat you wouldn't know about these things, but—'

'*How* powerful exactly?' India interrupted him, sounding worried.

'Extremely powerful,' Mephisto replied.

Tani started to speak then. 'You know, witch-babies' toenails were once used in a very famous robbery,' she said. 'Two witch-sisters who specialized in bad magic – the Broom sisters – used them to make a spell that deactivated the electronic tags that shops attach to their goods to prevent them being stolen.'

'The kind of tags that make that beeping noise if you try and leave the store?' India asked. (She had once spotted a very pretty silk scarf in a shop window, which she had thought would make an excellent sari, but when she had tried to drag it outside she had been deafened by the terrible beeping – and the loud laughter of the security guard. 'And to think I was going to leave them *two* live mice in exchange for it!' India had told Mephisto indignantly afterwards.)

'That's right,' Mephisto replied now. 'I remember the Broom sisters only too well. Belinda and Murdina Broom invented a

spell that helped them steal the entire contents of an indoor shopping centre. They were caught because someone saw them trying to transport a whole lot of stolen televisions home on their broomsticks. They got reported to the Good Witches' Society and they ended up in prison.'

'Bunty said she was going to report Spike's stolen toenails to the Good Witches' Society,' Cosmo said. 'Will they be able to catch who did it and get the toenails back again?'

Mephisto and Tani looked at each other. Hagnus and Matty noticed that their mother's tail was beginning to go slightly bushy at the tip – which only happened when she was very worried about something.

'I don't know,' Mephisto finally said.

'What will happen if they *can't* find the toenails?' Hagnus asked.

'I'm not sure, but if that many toenails have been stolen, I can't help thinking that whoever is behind this must be planning to use them for something big,' his mother replied. 'And since the toenails will have to be used while they are still glowing – that means they will have to be used *soon*.'

'Couldn't they have been stolen to sell on individually to other witches?' India asked. 'A single bag of witch-baby toenails would fetch quite a high price, by the sound of it.'

'Perhaps,' Tani agreed – but she didn't sound convinced.

'Well . . .' Meowface had stood up while they were talking and he was now walking towards the cat flap. 'Toenail robbery or no toenail robbery, *the show must go on*, as we say in the business! Perhaps you could show me the way to this school hall, Cosmo?'

'It's just down the road,' Cosmo replied. 'I can help you get inside if you like. Scarlett left her gloves in the cloakroom once and I snuck in through a broken window in the toilets to get them for her.'

'I'll come with you, Cosmo,' Mia said excitedly, but her mother quickly intervened.

'I don't believe you have finished your lessons for the day, Mia,' she told her sharply. 'I have a dead shrew at home that I want you to dissect.'

So Mia was forced to return home with her mother, and Tani took Hagnus and Matty home too. India said she was going to have a rest on Goody and Gabriel's bed, and Mephisto went with her.

That left Meowface and Cosmo alone together, and as the two of them set off

49

down the road towards Scarlett's school, Cosmo started to ask Meowface lots of questions about the legendary Cleo Cattrap.

'Is it true that he once had tea with the queen?' Cosmo wanted to know.

'He did visit Buckingham Palace once,' Meowface agreed. 'But the queen's corgis were so rude to him that he refused to stay for tea. I expect the queen was most disappointed not to meet him.'

'*I* can't wait to meet him,' Cosmo mewed in awe. 'Will you introduce me to him as soon as he gets here, Meowface?'

'Of course I will. And I shall tell him that it was you who found the venue for our catwalk. I'm sure he'll be *most* impressed.'

'Do you really think so?' Cosmo asked. And he was so excited that he started to race in circles around Meowface with his tail all bushed up.

4

The following day at the local Witch Prison, Sybil was waiting for her friend Selina Slaughter to arrive. As she sat in the prison visiting room, Sybil felt very cross as she thought about her old house – which had now been taken over by the Two-Shoes family – and her old witch-cat, Mephisto, who had served her faithfully until he had discovered that she was making bad spells instead of good ones. She longed to have both a house and a witch-cat of her own again, but most of all she longed to get her hands on that infuriating witch-kitten, Cosmo, who had totally wrecked her plans to use a brilliantly evil spell to become the richest witch in the world.

She was delighted when Selina arrived

and informed her that, not only had the toenail robbery been a great success, but one of the sets of toenails that Selina herself had stolen had belonged to Goody Two-Shoes's new baby son.

'The toenail robbery was perfectly coordinated using your excellent plan, Sybil,' Selina whispered to her now. 'Your mother would have been proud of you!' Sybil's mother had been the most evil of all the local witches before she had accidently ended up as a puff of green smoke after one of her evil spells had gone wrong.

'Once we have collected the other ingredient, we will be ready,' Sybil said. 'Then we will go down in history!' She cackled, but as she wasn't very good at cackling it came out as a rather loud croak.

The croaking noise reminded Selina of the downside of their plan. 'Of course if it were to go wrong for any reason . . .'

'. . . there will be a lot of very angry frogs hopping about,' Sybil finished for her. 'But it won't go wrong, Selina. My plan is perfect.'

'How does Murdina feel about you borrowing her spell recipe?' Selina asked.

'She's very excited. She says her sister, Belinda, would be excited too if she hadn't

got turned into a frog last year while she was trying to escape. Stupid woman! She should have waited!'

'So now that we've got the toenails, tell me how you want me to get the other ingredient,' Selina said, just as the bell went to signal the end of visiting time.

'You must find a place where lots of cats congregate together,' Sybil told her. 'And don't take too long about it. The magic in those toenails will only stay active for a very short time. We must have everything ready by next week at the latest.'

At the same time that Selina was visiting Sybil in prison, Cosmo and Mia were racing around Cosmo's front garden feeling very excited. Any minute now they were going to meet the legendary Cleo Cattrap! Meowface had just gone to collect him from the train station, where he had arrived that morning after spending a comfortable night in a spare bunk in a first-class carriage of the overnight sleeper train from Scotland. (Meowface himself had travelled south on the same train two days previously, on a slightly more humble seat on top of a suitcase on a luggage rack.)

Since Meowface had heard that Cosmo's house was due to be free of its two-legged occupants for at least another few days, he had suggested that Cleo Cattrap might wish to stay with them during his visit.

'He often prefers the comfort of a family home – however humble – to the richer trappings of fine hotels,' Meowface had told Mephisto.

'Does he really?' Mephisto had replied, with just a hint of a growl in his throat. But India had said that of course he could stay

55

and Mephisto had agreed, although he hadn't seemed nearly as pleased about it as Cosmo and India were. Cosmo couldn't understand his father sometimes – after all, it wasn't every day that one of the most famous cats in the country came to stay with you, was it?

As Cosmo and Mia waited in the front garden, India and Mephisto were attending a lecture at Felina's house, where the professor-cat was offering advice to a group of cats whose humans (or witches) had just had new babies. Mia's mother had a personal interest in this topic. As a very young kitten she had arrived in her first human household at the same time as a new baby – and as a consequence had received very little fuss from her humans, who were far too distracted by their baby. She had decided to leave and had presented herself at the doors of the local cat-rescue centre, where she had spent a period of two weeks carefully vetting every human who came in to look for a pet. Finally she had picked Amy – and had easily secured her chosen placement by rushing up to her and giving her so much affection that Amy's heart was immediately won over. Felina did understand, however, that most cats didn't actually want to leave their homes when a new baby arrived, and she had therefore worked out a special training programme that cats could apply to their humans instead.

'Look, Cosmo, they're coming!' Mia mewed excitedly, standing up on her hind legs in order to look over the wall and out on to the street where Meowface and a long-haired grey Persian cat could be seen sauntering up the road together.

'I'll go and fetch Mother and Father,'

57

Cosmo replied, racing across into Mia's front garden and hurtling round to access the cat flap at the back of the house.

Inside the kitchen, Professor Felina was perched on the table, surrounded by twenty or so other cats who were all sitting on the floor, listening to her. 'Even humans or witches who have already been trained to put their cat's needs before their own,' she was declaring solemnly, 'may change their behaviour when a baby enters the household.'

'My witch makes me sleep downstairs now, instead of on her bed at night!' an indignant black witch-cat shouted out.

'My human screamed at me when I jumped into the baby's pram to have a nap,' a fat tabby cat added.

Cosmo completely forgot about Cleo Cattrap for a moment and raised his paw to ask a question. 'What about witch-children?' he asked. 'Do they forget all about us when they get a new baby brother or sister?'

'Children are very wise, thank goodness,' Felina told him. 'It doesn't take them long to see that cats – especially kittens – still make much better playmates than new babies.'

Cosmo felt his mother's warm tongue lick him on the top of his head as she came to stand behind him. 'Scarlett will always love you and want to play with you, Cosmo. Don't worry about that. And I expect when baby Spike gets older, he will love you too.'

Cosmo gave a relieved little purr, then he mewed quickly, 'Mother, I've come to let you know that Cleo Cattrap is here.'

Mephisto gave a soft growl when he heard this news. He had persisted in being relatively unenthusiastic about having the great Cleo Cattrap as their guest, and he had

59

already made it clear that Meowface must
sleep at Tani's house. ('*One* other male cat
sharing my territory is the absolute limit,' he
had told India firmly.)

India looked a little worried as she followed Mephisto out of the cat flap, with
Cosmo close on her tail.

Mephisto halted abruptly as they rounded
the corner of the house and saw Cleo standing there with Meowface and an awestruck
Mia.

'He's not nearly as handsome as everyone
makes out,' Mephisto commented to India,
stopping to lick his front paw nonchalantly
before strolling forward at a very leisurely
pace to greet their guest.

Cosmo, however, was totally thrilled by
the large, long-haired, hazel-eyed grey and
white Persian cat he saw in front of him.
India seemed quite excited too and she

whispered to Cosmo, 'Persian cats usually have short noses, but Cleo has quite a long one – I think that makes him even *more* good-looking, don't you?'

Before Cosmo had time to reply, India had set off across the lawn after Mephisto, and Cosmo noticed that Cleo Cattrap immediately stopped looking at Mephisto to give his full attention to India. Mia, who was overcome with shyness, had moved away to sit behind a nearby bush.

Cosmo half ran, half tumbled over the grass in order to get closer to Cleo himself, but he knew better than to overtake his father. Instead, he lay down on his belly beside his mother, who had also wisely halted, and the two of them watched from a safe distance away as the two male cats formally greeted each other. The two stood face to face for a few moments, with their

61

whiskers in the forward position, before
Mephisto began to walk around Cleo in a
circle, growling and keeping his ears
flattened the whole time.

'Welcome, Cleo Cattrap,' Mephisto
finally said gruffly. 'I must say it's been a
while since I've met a grey Persian. And I see
you've got a stripy head as well!'

For the first time Cleo spoke. His voice

was throaty and rather posh as he replied, 'I am a long-haired silver-tabby Persian. *Silver*, not grey.'

'How interesting,' Mephisto replied crisply. 'So you've got a bit of tabby-cat in you as well, have you?'

'Tabby *Persian*,' Cleo corrected him, narrowing his eyes.

'Of course . . . well . . . you are welcome to sleep on the pile of washing in our utility room tonight. I'm sure you will find it comfortable enough.'

'I'm afraid I shall have to sleep on a proper mattress,' Cleo declared immediately. 'Otherwise I won't get a *wink*. We pedigree cats are more delicate creatures than you moggies, I'm afraid.'

Mephisto seemed about to hiss back in response, when India quickly intervened. 'That won't be a problem, will it, Mephisto?

After all there are plenty of spare beds now that we have the house to ourselves.'

'How kind!' Cleo exclaimed, turning towards her and purring very loudly. 'Perhaps you'd care to show me, my dear.'

But before Cleo could move any closer to India, Mephisto had stepped in between them. '*I'll* show you,' he said firmly. 'India needs to rest. She is carrying nine of my kittens, you know. Cosmo – please show Meowface the way to Tani's house.'

'Oh, don't worry about that,' said Meowface, who had been standing well back as Cleo and Mephisto were formally introduced. 'I already know where my cousin lives. Right now I need to find a suitable restaurant for us to have our lunch.'

'A *restaurant*?' India looked amazed.

'Cleo and I always eat out whenever we can,' Meowface explained. 'We especially like fish restaurants. Would you care to join us?'

India stared at him. 'But only humans and witches eat in restaurants,' she said. 'Not *cats*.'

But Meowface just laughed. 'I'll be back here to fetch you all in half an hour.' And he licked his lips in anticipation before hurrying off.

65

5

Cosmo said goodbye to Mia and followed his parents and Cleo Cattrap into the house, where his father took Cleo upstairs to show him the beds. It didn't take Cleo long to find the room with the newest bed, which was smaller than the others and had strange wooden sides to it. A pile of soft blankets and a snugly quilt were neatly folded on top of the mattress and Cleo instantly selected it as the perfect bed for himself.

'It seems almost as if it was designed especially for me,' Cleo said, as he leaped up on to a chair, ready to jump over the wooden slatted side.

But Mephisto soon objected. 'India might need this bed when she has my kittens,' he said gruffly. 'It looks like a very good nesting place.'

'Except that it won't be very easy for me to get in and out of it,' India pointed out. 'Let Cleo sleep there if he wants to, Mephisto. I've already selected the place where I want to give birth. Come and see.'

So, as Cleo made himself comfortable on his new bed, India led Mephisto into the room where Scarlett's parents usually slept, to show him a large oval-shaped basket with a handle on each side. It had a padded bottom with a clean white sheet covering it, and a soft white blanket spread out on top of that.

What is it?' Cosmo asked curiously.

'The other day I heard Goody call it a Moses basket,' India said.

'It's clearly an especially large and comfortable type of cat basket,' Mephisto

67

replied. 'How thoughtful.' He climbed inside to test it out, and he was still there half an hour later when they heard a loud miaow coming from outside.

Meowface had returned.

Curious to know if he had managed to find a restaurant that served lunch to cats, Cosmo and his parents headed downstairs to find that Cleo had already joined Meowface in the garden.

'There's a sushi restaurant just a ten-minute walk away from here,' Meowface told them.

'Sushi is my favourite,' Cleo told them, purring loudly.

'What *is* sushi?' Cosmo asked.

'It's a special kind of Japanese food that has lots of fish in it,' Meowface explained. 'The fish is served in tiny cat-sized pieces, on little mounds of rice. It's quite delicious.'

'But how are we going to get them to serve *us*?' India asked. 'And how will we pay for it?'

'We'll serve ourselves,' Meowface said, 'and we'll lick the dishes clean for them afterwards – that will be payment enough. Now, follow me.'

So Cleo, Mephisto, India and Cosmo all

69

followed Meowface down the road towards the local high street, where the sushi restaurant was situated.

'Shouldn't we use the customers' entrance at the front?' India asked, as Meowface led them into the little yard at the back of the building.

'We're *special* customers,' Meowface said. 'Now . . . if you'll just wait here while I grab hold of my little helper . . .' He leaped up and knocked the lid off a metal dustbin that was standing outside the back door. It was clearly empty – or at least not very full – because he was able to jump right inside it. A lot of miaowing and squeaking followed.

'Has he got a mouse in there?' Cosmo burst out in surprise. Although cats and mice spoke different languages, most cats understood enough mouse language to be

70

able to have a basic conversation, and vice versa.

Meowface's cross voice could be heard inside the bin. 'I keep telling you – you'll be *quite* safe! Stop making such a fuss or we'll have *you* for our lunch instead!'

That seemed to end the squeaking, and Meowface called out to the other cats, 'I always think mice are far more useful alive than dead – unless one is *very* hungry of course!' Then he jumped out of the bin and they saw that he was carrying a mouse in his jaws. It was actually rather a handsome mouse, with white fur, a long tail and pink eyes, and Meowface was holding it very carefully so as not to squash it.

Cleo Cattrap, who had obviously been witness to this routine before, immediately started yowling at the top of his voice before thumping his hind legs as loudly as

11

he could against
the back door of
the restaurant.

The door was
soon opened by a
cross-looking
human in a white
apron, and Meow-
face immediately
darted inside with
the mouse still between his jaws.

'He'll let it loose in the restaurant and all
the customers will run away,' Cleo told the
other cats, confidently leading the way in
through the door which the human had left
open in his rush to follow Meowface. 'Then
we can jump up on to the tables and finish
everything on their plates.'

'Won't the waiters stop us?' India asked.

'The mouse will run into the kitchen after

it's scared everyone out of the restaurant,' Cleo said. 'All the staff will be too busy trying to catch it to notice us.'

Screams could now be heard coming from the restaurant and it was clear that Meowface had let go of the mouse. There was complete chaos as everybody vacated the restaurant area, and the staff rushed around trying to calm down their customers and catch the mouse at the same time.

'Mice always cause much more of a stir in restaurants than cats do,' Meowface said as they joined him under one of the tables. 'I don't know why that is, but it's very useful. We'll have to eat fast though. I have a feeling that mouse will head straight for the back door instead of running twice round the kitchen like I told him to.'

As soon as all the customers had gone and the waiters had disappeared into the kitchen

73

after the mouse, the cats jumped up on to the tables and began to eat. Meowface had been right about there being lots of little mounds of rice, most of which had pieces of fish on top. And the pieces of fish were just the right size for a cat to eat in one mouthful.

They had scarcely finished eating when a

waiter came back into the dining area, took one look at the cats feasting on the remains of his customers' lunches and started to yell.

'This way!' Meowface shouted, leaping across three tables to reach one by an open window, which he had already identified as their escape route.

'Shouldn't we make sure the mouse got away safely?' India said in a worried voice, as they hurried towards home. (Cosmo's mother was known for her kindness to smaller creatures, with the possible exception of goldfish, which she just couldn't resist snacking on.)

'Oh, I wouldn't worry about *him*,' Meowface said dismissively. 'He'll be halfway home by now.'

But that was where he was wrong. The mouse in question *had* escaped from the restaurant, but instead of making for home

15

he was now following at a safe distance behind them. He was actually one of several white mice who worked as spies for Selina Slaughter, and it was no coincidence that he had been in the backyard of the restaurant at the same time as Meowface. He had gone there deliberately, because he had heard a rumour that Cleo Cattrap was in town – and Cleo Cattrap was known to favour restaurants that served fish. If Cleo was there it must mean that he was planning to hold one of his famous Catwalk Extravaganzas, and that was the reason the mouse wanted to find him. Selina Slaughter had sent out all her spies with instructions that a large piece of cheese was going to be awarded to the one who found the place where the largest number of cats was due to congregate together within the next few days.

On their way home the cats passed

Scarlett's school. 'This is the place where we're going to hold the competition,' Meowface told Cleo. 'Come and have a closer look.' As he led Cleo in through the school gates, the cats had absolutely no idea that they were being spied on by the white mouse, who followed them right across the school playground and round to the back of the building.

'That's where we can get inside,' Meowface said to Cleo, pointing out the broken toilet window (which was just the right size to admit a cat). 'The school hall will be the perfect venue for the catwalk competition. Do you want to come inside now and see what you think?'

'Let's come back later,' Cleo said, yawning. 'I think an afternoon nap is in order first. That really was an extremely heavy lunch.'

So Meowface agreed that they could return to inspect the hall together in a couple of hours' time, and the mouse, having overheard this, let out a satisfied squeak and scurried away.

Later that afternoon, when they had all enjoyed a restful post-lunch nap, Meowface announced that he was taking Cleo back to the school. He asked Cosmo if he would like to go with them, and Cosmo immediately went to find Mia to see if she wanted to come too.

Inside the school assembly hall, which doubled as a gym when the children had PE, Cleo walked around slowly, nodding approvingly at the size of it, and at the gym mats, which could be arranged across the floor to provide soft seating for all the spectators. He especially liked the fact that a

19

long wooden bench had been left out in the middle of the hall instead of being stacked away properly at the end of term.

'This can be our catwalk,' he declared, jumping on top of it and walking along it himself.

Then he excused himself and disappeared off to the toilets to have a look at himself in the mirror.

Meowface quickly explained to Mia and Cosmo that Cleo liked to look at himself in front of a mirror at least once every day, and that he must never be disturbed during those times.

'I'll tell you a secret if you promise to keep it to yourselves,' Meowface added, lowering his voice to a level that was no louder than a whisper (which was quite a difficult thing for a cat who was a quarter Siamese to do). 'He's got a bit of a thing about his nose not being as short as a Persian cat's ought to be, and I reckon that's why he's always looking in the mirror – because deep down he's really insecure about his appearance.'

'Mother noticed his nose was quite long,' Cosmo said, 'but *she* thinks it makes him more attractive. Would it help if I told him that, do you think?'

'Oh no,' Meowface said quickly. 'You must never mention his nose, Cosmo. He'll throw a hissy fit if you do! You see, he *tells* everyone he's a pure-bred, silver-tabby Persian with a pedigree as long as your tail, but what nobody else knows is that one of his grandfathers was actually an alley cat. That's why Cleo's nose is longer than other Persians'. And he's so jealous of all pure-bred Persian cats with short noses that he won't let any so much as *enter* his catwalk competitions, let alone win them!' Meowface

81

stopped talking abruptly as Cleo reappeared, carrying something quite bulky between his jaws.

As he came closer, they saw that it was a cat-sized bouquet of flowers. He dropped it on the floor and miaowed, 'Someone must have thrown this in through the window for me. Look – there's a message attached.'

The 'message' was a wriggling white mouse that had been tied to the bouquet by its tail, and Cosmo, Mia and Meowface all stared at it.

The mouse looked quite similar to the one they had met at lunchtime. 'I bring greetings from my mistress,' it said, doing its best to squeak slowly so the cats could understand it, but not succeeding very well. (Most mice found it difficult not to squeak very rapidly whenever they were in conversation with a cat.) 'My mistress is a huge admirer of the great Cleo Cattrap and she wishes to invite him to partake of a most delicious tea,' it told them.

Cleo looked at the mouse and licked his lips, at which point it quickly squealed, '*I'm* not the tea. The tea's at *her* house!'

'Perhaps she means the mouse to be the appetizer,' Meowface suggested.

'Oh no!' The mouse's squeak was even more high-pitched now. '*My* job is to take you to where she lives! She has sent me here on her broomstick to fetch you.'

'Who *is* your mistress?' Cosmo asked curiously.

83

'I'm not allowed to tell you her name. She says it would spoil the surprise.'

'I wouldn't go with him if I were you,' Meowface told Cleo. 'You've never ridden on a broomstick before. What if you fall off?'

'There's a basket attached – you can sit in that,' the mouse quickly responded.

'I still don't think you should go,' Meowface said. 'Not if you don't know where he's taking you.'

'You should never go *anywhere* with a stranger,' Cosmo agreed.

But Cleo ignored both of them. 'This mistress of yours is a great admirer of mine, you say?'

'Oh yes,' the mouse squeaked eagerly. 'She greatly admires you for your cleverness and your refined taste in all things, but most of all for your handsome appearance. She

84

wants you to come and have tea with her, so she can tell you all these things herself.'

Cleo found himself purring rather loudly – he liked nothing better than a good dose of flattery. 'Well . . .' he miaowed. 'Perhaps, I *will* come. Meowface, I want you to find some other helpers and have this hall ready for the competition by the time I get back.' He glanced at Cosmo and Mia. 'You two kittens can spread the word that I'll be starting my auditions here tomorrow morning at sunrise.' With an extra-grand swoosh of his fluffy grey tail, he added, 'And make sure you tell everyone that what Cleo Cattrap is looking for in this competition is the F factor. Nothing less will do!'

After he had gone, Cosmo said, 'Wow! The F factor! If only *I* had that!'

'According to Mother, *all* cats do,' Mia mewed.

85

'I mean the sort of F factor that Cleo is talking about,' Cosmo said. 'The sort that would make you really stand out from the crowd!'

'You *do* stand out from the crowd, Cosmo,' Mia told him earnestly.

Cosmo gave her head an affectionate lick and said, 'I wish *we* could enter this competition.'

'You *can* enter it – as long as you get your parents' permission first,' Meowface told them. 'There's a special category for kittens.'

'*Really?*' Cosmo's tail began to go bushy with excitement as he mewed, 'Come on, Mia! Let's go and ask them right now!'

Felina was studying a new book when the two kittens arrived at Mia's house. It was a large book that Amy had got out of the library and it was all about a country called

China, which Felina told them was even further away than India.

'Look, Mia!' Felina miaowed excitedly as she showed her daughter some Chinese writing, which seemed to be made up of lots of complicated combinations of strokes rather than the more rounded letters Mia was used to seeing when her mother forced her to read human English. 'This would be very easy for a cat to write.' And Felina demonstrated by making several complex scratches on the back of Amy's leather sofa, which she told them meant *Hello* in Chinese.

'Mother, we've just found out that kittens are allowed to enter the catwalk competition,' Mia began timidly, 'so I was wondering if—'

But Felina interrupted before she could finish. 'Mia, I forbid you to have anything to do with that ridiculous beauty contest. This afternoon we are both going to use our *brains*!' She turned to Cosmo, who was slowly shrinking backwards towards the door. 'Cosmo, would *you* like to learn how to write in Chinese too?'

'Err . . . No thanks,' Cosmo mewed politely. 'See you later, Mia.' He gave his friend a sympathetic look as he hurried away.

Cosmo didn't think he would have the same difficulty as Mia in getting his parents to let him enter the catwalk competition. He had frequently overheard Mephisto and India congratulating themselves on having produced the most beautiful kitten in the neighbourhood, so he couldn't imagine them minding if he wanted to enter a competition to show himself off.

But he had reckoned without his father's dislike of Cleo Cattrap.

'He's left his disgusting grey hairs all over my favourite seat,' Mephisto was complaining to India when Cosmo bounded in through the cat flap. 'I told you I didn't want him taking his nap there after lunch. And I'm sure he's got fleas.'

89

'Well, so have you. I saw one on you just the other day.'

'Nonsense! I'd know if I had a flea. I'd be itchy.' Just at that moment Mephisto felt very itchy just behind his left ear, and it took all his willpower not to lift up his back leg to scratch it.

So it was very bad timing on Cosmo's part when he shouted out excitedly, 'Mother! Father! Guess what? Meowface says that *kittens* are allowed to enter the catwalk competition! We just have to get our parents' permission first.'

Mephisto sniffed as if he was highly irritated. 'Who does Cleo Cattrap think he is to set himself up as a judge over all us other cats? Cosmo, I will definitely *not* allow you to enter!'

'But that's not fair—' Cosmo began to

yowl, at which point his mother quickly intervened.

'Don't raise your voice like that to your father,' she told him. 'Now go outside and play. Your father and I need to talk.'

So Cosmo grumpily headed back outside, wondering what to do next. He didn't feel much like going to spread the word about the catwalk competition all on his own. Then he remembered his other friends, Hagnus and Matty. They would probably come with him if he asked. 'I bet *they'll* be allowed to enter the competition,' he grumbled to himself as he set off towards Tani's house with his tail swishing crossly behind him.

6

Cosmo and his two Siamese friends toured the neighbourhood for the remainder of the afternoon, causing quite a stir as they spread the news that Cleo Cattrap's auditions were to start the next day at sunrise. It was early evening by the time they returned to the school hall where Tani, along with several other adult cats, had gone to help Meowface. All the mats had been dragged into position, and an upturned cardboard box had been placed in the centre of the room, from where Cleo could sit and judge all the contestants.

Cleo had not long arrived back himself and had gone straight to the toilets to look at himself in the mirror *again*.

'He hasn't told us yet who his mysterious

admirer is,' Meowface said to Cosmo. 'He seems very excited since he came back from seeing her though. He says he's got something to tell us all in a minute about the entry fee.'

'*What* entry fee?' Cosmo asked.

'Every cat who enters one of his competitions has to pay an entry fee of some sort. Usually it's something edible.' He stopped talking as Cleo himself came into the room.

'Meowface, I have decided that the entry fee for this particular competition will be one hairball per cat,' Cleo said. 'You must tell everyone this when they turn up tomorrow morning. Tell them that no cat will be permitted to audition unless they have given me a hairball and that I will postpone the start of the competition to allow time for this.'

'What's a hairball?' Cosmo asked,

93

wondering if it was some sort of cat toy that he hadn't yet heard of.

'It's a ball of hair that you bring up of course,' Hagnus said.

'Huh?' Cosmo still didn't understand.

'It's a ball of fur that sits in your stomach until you sick it up,' Matty explained. 'It's quite normal – all cats have them. The more you groom yourself by licking your fur clean, the more fur you swallow and the more hairballs you get. If you want to bring one up you should go and chew some grass. Grass is especially good for making you regurgitate whatever's in your stomach.'

Now Cosmo remembered the soggy lumps that India sometimes brought up on the carpet. She always made a noise a bit like a coffee percolator whenever she was about to deposit one. And come to think of it, they often contained bits of grass.

'Mother never told me those things were called hairballs,' he said. 'And I've never had one myself.'

'That's probably because your mother still grooms you all the time,' Matty explained. 'You only get them if you lick your fur a lot. Our mother's started letting Hagnus and me wash ourselves, so now we've been getting them too.'

Cleo suddenly let out a loud miaow and it was clear that he wished to make an additional announcement. 'I almost forgot. These hairballs must be completely free of fleas.'

'But that's ridiculous,' Meowface protested. 'It's a well-known fact that fleas and cat fur sometimes get swallowed together.' Meowface himself had a lot of fleas and he knew that in the course of washing himself, he couldn't help but occasionally swallow one or two.

'Anyway, how can you tell if there's a flea inside a hairball or not?' Tani wanted to know.

'I have just been lent a special magic device that can detect them,' Cleo said. 'It's called a flea detector. I shall test each hairball personally and the detector will beep if it picks up the presence of a flea.'

'What are you going to *do* with all these hairballs?' Tani wanted to know.

Cleo looked sly. 'That is none of your business,' he told her. 'Now if you'll excuse me, I have to go and rest before tomorrow's auditions.'

Cosmo went straight to Mia's house to tell his friend the news about the entry fee, and it turned out that Mia knew exactly what a hairball was. 'Mother used to get them all the time until Amy started feeding us anti-hairball cat food to stop her bringing them up on the carpet. Amy makes a terrible fuss about anything we bring up on the carpet.'

'It doesn't look as if we've got *any* chance of being in this competition now,' Cosmo said gloomily. 'Even if your mother and my father change their minds about letting us enter, we don't have any hairballs for the entry fee.'

'There's no way Mother will change her mind in any case,' Mia said, sighing.

'I don't think my father will either,' Cosmo said, 'but let's start washing ourselves as much as we can from now on, just in case. And we must make sure we swallow as much hair as possible with each lick.'

The subject of cat hairballs was also being discussed that evening, in a phone conversation between Sybil (who was allowed to

make one phone call from prison every week) and her friend Selina Slaughter.

'That's splendid news!' Sybil was exclaiming triumphantly as Selina told her about the catwalk competition. 'Cats who are entering a beauty contest will groom themselves even more than usual – which means they'll produce nice fat hairballs. And as soon as we have those hairballs, we'll have everything we need for the spell.'

'I've lent my wand with a flea-detector spell in it to that puffed up fluff-ball of a cat who runs the competition,' Selina told her.

'Are you sure he knows how to use it properly?' Sybil asked. 'He sounds like a very stupid cat to me.'

'He's more vain than stupid,' Selina replied. 'That's why it was so easy to fool him. But when I showed him how to use the flea detector – which is what I told him it was – he didn't seem to have a problem with it.'

'Good, because according to Murdina Broom, a single flea will render the hairball it's in completely useless,' Sybil told her. 'And we know what that will mean for the witch concerned.'

Selina made a croaking sound, which was meant as a joke, but which Sybil didn't find at all funny.

'Believe me, Selina, this is no laughing matter!'

'Of course not, Sybil,' Selina put in

99

hastily. 'But don't worry. Nothing can go wrong. And just think . . . After this we'll be able to set up an Evil Witches' Society that will be even more powerful than the Good Witches' one. All the witches you've helped escape will be in your debt. Of course, if you didn't have me helping you on the outside—'

'Don't worry, Selina,' Sybil reassured her. '*You* will be handsomely rewarded too. Once I escape, you and I are going to be the richest and most powerful witches in the country! But there's just one more thing I need you to do, Selina, my dear. I'll need my broomstick ready for me the second I escape. I left it in the garage of my old house and I was hoping that—'

'I'll do a spell to summon it,' Selina said quickly. 'Don't worry, I'll make sure it's waiting for you. But, Sybil, how are we going to make sure that you and the others don't all get recaptured and sent back to prison again straight away?'

'Because we'll make sure that the good witches are too busy to come looking for us. This toenail robbery hasn't just provided us with the spell ingredient we needed, it's given us lots and lots of poor little witch-babies who have no magic toenails to protect them against evil spells. So after we escape we'll make sure we sprinkle *lots* of nasty spells into the air – spells that are especially targeted at babies! The good witches will be too busy protecting them to start chasing after us. And by the time the babies are out of danger, we'll be long gone.'

'Perfect!' Selina said, giggling. 'And Murdina Broom is a whizz when it comes to knocking up evil spells against babies. Why, one time I remember—'

'I know how good she is,' Sybil interrupted, lowering her voice to a whisper. 'And if our escape plan is successful, she's promised to do me a special little favour in return for all my hard work. I've asked her to make me a spell that targets baby *cats*.'

'But, Sybil—'

'Any witch who harms a cat will end up as a puff of green smoke, blah, blah, blah . . . That's what Murdina said too. But I've told her that's just a load of superstitious nonsense!'

'But, Sybil, it's *not* nonsense! What about your mother? Didn't you say that was how she—?'

'Selina, my dear, you are much cleverer than Murdina so I may as well come clean with you. As you and I both know, most witches *are* affected by the ancient curse that forbids witches to harm cats. My mother

102

certainly was! But I have human blood in me, which mean I am more powerful than other witches. I certainly *can* harm cats and get away with it. Why else do you think that pesky Cosmo is so afraid of me? In fact, if there's ever any cat that *you* want to get rid of, Selina, you are welcome to ask for my help!' She chuckled. 'Now . . . I've managed to persuade Murdina that no harm will come to her if she gives me a special ready-made spell that I can put into action all on my own.'

'What kind of spell?' Selina asked curiously.

'The unmentionably evil kind of course! And it's going to be heading in the direction of my least favourite kitten – and all the other kittens I've heard his stuck-up mother is about to give birth to.'

'You mean—?' Selina broke off, overcome

by a mixture of dumb admiration and total disbelief.

'If this spell works,' Sybil cackled, 'I shall be out of prison along with all the other witches – and the only ones who'll be getting turned into frogs will be pesky Cosmo and his family!'

7

The following morning Scarlett's school hall was crammed with cats. There were big cats and small cats, alley cats and house cats, moggy cats and pedigree cats, witch-cats and non witch-cats. Most of the cats were fully grown but there were also quite a few kittens, including Cosmo, Mia, Matty and Hagnus. The two Siamese kittens had already been given permission to enter the competition by their mother, who was also going to take part.

Cleo himself was standing on top of one of the sinks in the toilets, staring at himself in the mirror. He had just spent over an hour grooming his long, slightly tangled fur when he had noticed that a hand-dryer was fixed to the wall and that a stool had been placed just underneath it. He had realized that if he jumped up on to the stool he could stand on his hind legs and reach the button that switched on the dryer. So that was what he had done – his fur was wet from the intensive licking he had given it and he needed to dry off.

Finding the electric dryer had set Cleo thinking about his past. A long time ago, when he had been little more than a kitten, he had had his fur shampooed regularly by his first human family, who had blow-dried it very carefully each time. Cleo had relished all the attention, and even now the sound of a hairdryer always gave him a warm glow inside. But his humans had wanted to show him off at cat shows, and when they had realized that his nose was too long to win any prizes they had given him away to another family instead. Cleo's second family

hadn't minded about his nose, but they hadn't bothered to shampoo him or dry him with a hairdryer – in fact they had treated him just like any other cat. And that was when Cleo had decided to run away and set up his own catwalk show, where *he* would be the judge of who was a prize-winning cat and who wasn't. And he had vowed that he would *never*, under any circumstances, allow flat-faced Persian cats with short noses to enter any of *his* competitions.

But soon, Cleo told himself, none of that was going to matter any more. And he found himself purring with pleasure as he remembered the thing that Selina Slaughter had promised to do for him in return for all the hairballs he was going to give her.

In the assembly hall the throng of waiting cats was getting restless, and impatient mutterings of, 'Where is he then?' could be heard around the room.

'We shouldn't really be here,' Mia was mewing to Cosmo nervously. 'What if our parents find out?'

'They just said we weren't allowed to *enter* the competition,' Cosmo pointed out. 'They didn't say we weren't allowed to come and watch.'

Meowface suddenly jumped up on to the upturned box where Cleo was due to sit in a few moments, and called out loudly for silence. 'I need to let you know about the entry fee before Cleo comes to tell you about the competition,' he miaowed, in such a loud voice that even the cats at the very back of the hall could hear him quite easily. 'The entry fee for this competition is one hairball per cat. When you have delivered this you

109

will be admitted to the auditions. The auditions will start at this time tomorrow.'

'But I thought the auditions were today,' someone mewed.

'Cleo is postponing them until tomorrow, to allow you time to bring up your hairballs. Oh – and you must make sure they don't have any fleas in them.'

A surprised murmur went round the room, especially from the more flea-ridden cats in the audience.

'I know it's tricky but you'll just have to watch where you're licking,' Meowface said. 'Now . . . will everyone please give a big welcome to the host of this competition . . . Yes . . . it's the cat you've all been waiting to meet . . . it's the one and only . . . *Cleo Cattrap!*'

A lot of catcalling filled the room as Cleo finally appeared in the doorway of the

110

assembly hall. Cleo waited for the other cats to step back and create a passage for him, then he walked into the room, swinging his hindquarters extra-elegantly and holding his chin up as high as it would go as he drank in the welcome he was receiving. His own entrance was always his favourite part of every catwalk competition.

Finally he reached the upturned box, which Meowface had now vacated, and jumped up on top of it. He waited until his audience became silent before addressing them in his most refined voice.

'I am delighted that so many of you have come to audition for my Amazing Catwalk Extravaganza!' he announced. 'The auditions will start tomorrow, but today I will tell you what I am looking for in my winning cats.' He paused dramatically, twitching his whiskers as he scanned the crowd of eager feline faces. 'I am looking for none other than the F factor!' he boomed out. 'I am looking for the ultimate in feline beauty, poise, hygiene, personality and vocal ability! That means that only cats with the shiniest coats, the most attractive ears, the best posture, the brightest eyes, the most tuneful miaows, the sweetest-smelling bottoms and the fishiest breaths will be picked to enter my catwalk competition.' He pointed out the catwalk itself, which some of his audience seemed surprised to see was just the school bench that had been left in the middle of the floor. 'On the day of the competition I will choose the three winners,' Cleo continued, 'and the cat who comes First will be crowned catwalk king . . . or queen,' he added quickly, as six rather large female cats in the front row started to hiss.

113

'What are the prizes?' one cat shouted out.

'The First Prize,' Cleo began grandly, 'is a luxury weekend break at an award-winning cat hotel. The winner will be fed three delicious meals each day and will sleep in a fully-heated basket on top of a goose-down duvet. There will be an inside toilet, regular grooming, and continual stroking and fussing by fully trained human staff.'

'That sounds wonderful!' Mia whispered to Cosmo, and the purrs of approval could be heard all around the hall.

'Second Prize,' Cleo continued, 'is a meal for two at a top fish restaurant – my friend Meowface will organize that. And Third Prize is a box of fish fingers.'

All the cats in the room were clearly well satisfied with the description of the prizes, and Cleo had to shout to be heard above all the excited mews as he added, 'There is also a special prize for the winning kitten under twelve months old. The winner of that category will receive a brand-new toy mouse from the local pet store. But all kittens must have the permission of their parents in order to take part.'

Now everyone in the room was happy – except Cosmo and Mia. 'It's not fair that we aren't allowed to enter!' Mia said grumpily.

Just then they heard a familiar miaow, and turned to see India standing behind them.

'Mother!' Cosmo mewed in alarm. 'What are *you* doing here?'

'I'm beginning to wonder that myself. It was quite a feat squeezing through that tiny window in my present condition, even if your father did give me a push from behind.'

'*Father's* here too?' Cosmo burst out, looking even more worried.

115

'Cosmo and I only came to watch, not to take part,' Mia put in quickly. '*My* mother isn't here as well, is she?'

India's eyes looked twinkly, as if she was feeling very amused by something. 'Actually, she is – but don't worry. I've managed to get Mephisto and Felina to change their minds about letting you enter the competition.'

'How?' Cosmo and Mia burst out together.

'First I had a little word with Cleo,' India said. 'You see, he's made himself rather comfortable in our house, and when I hinted that we *might* not be able to let him stay for much longer unless he agreed to my suggestion, that seemed to do the trick.'

'What suggestion?' Cosmo asked.

'To have more than one judge for this competition,' India replied.

Just then, Cleo started to speak again. 'I have one last announcement,' he began. 'For this competition – and *only* this competition – I have appointed two other judges as well as myself. They are both cats of high standing in the local community – or so I'm told . . . Professor Felina . . . Witch-cat Mephisto . . . will you please come and introduce yourselves?'

Cosmo and Mia could hardly believe their eyes as their respective parents jumped

up on to the upturned box, one after the
other, to wave a paw at the audience.

'I thought Mother *hated* beauty contests!'
Mia gasped.

'And I thought Father *hated* anything to
do with Cleo Cattrap!'

India was looking very pleased with herself. 'I managed to persuade both of them that
they could raise the standard of the competition by agreeing to be judges,' she explained.
'Actually, Mephisto didn't need much

persuading. And now he doesn't mind you entering the competition after all, Cosmo.'

'What about Mother?' Mia asked quickly.

'Your mother says you may enter the competition too, Mia – as long as you don't show her up by getting overexcited and chasing your tail.' (Mia chased her tail a lot, which her mother thought was not only silly, but also most unfitting behaviour for the daughter of such a clever professor-cat.)

So Mia started to chase *Cosmo's* tail instead of her own, as she raced round him in excitement.

Now all they had to do was bring up a hairball each, but they soon discovered that producing hairballs was much easier miaowed than done.

For the rest of that day, Cosmo and Mia found that no matter how much grass they chewed, and how much of their own (and

each other's) fur they licked, they couldn't seem to bring up even the tiniest hairball. They both felt even more frustrated when they learned that Hagnus and Matty had easily brought up one each (which they were guarding closely) and that their mother, Tani, had also produced one.

Cosmo finally decided to ask his own mother for help, and India spent the last hour before bedtime trying to teach her kitten how to bring things up on the living-room carpet. But although Cosmo did eventually manage to bring up all the Crunchie-munchies he had eaten for his supper, there was no sign of the hairball he so desperately needed.

'It must be because *I've* always washed you so much until now,' India said. 'All your loose fur is probably inside my tummy rather than yours. I'll tell you what – I'll see if *I* can bring one up. It will be a mixture of my fur *and* yours, and even a bit of your father's, but I'm sure it will do.'

'Will there be any fleas in it, do you think?' Cosmo asked anxiously, thinking of all the scratching he had seen his father doing lately.

'Of course not,' India said indignantly. 'I am very particular about not swallowing anything that jumps. Now stand back and I'll see what I can do.' And she began to make a glug-glug-glugging noise, just like a coffee-machine, as her tummy started to heave in and out.

The next morning at sunrise, Meowface was waiting in the school toilets, greeting each cat as it entered through the broken window. Most cats were carrying hairballs between their teeth. Meowface had managed to find a plastic bucket, into which he was asking

121

everyone to deposit their entry fee before they went through to the assembly hall. Only a few cats had turned up without hairballs, and Meowface had instructed them to wait in the toilet block instead of proceeding through to the main hall with the others.

Tani, Matty and Hagnus each dropped a hairball into the bucket and were allowed through. Then it was Cosmo and Mia's turn. Cosmo now had a large hairball which his mother had produced for him last night, but Mia still hadn't managed to get herself one. Her mother had tried to help her but had failed miserably – a fact Felina blamed on the new anti-hairball cat food Amy had been feeding them recently.

'Meowface, can't you just let this be Mia's entry fee as well?' Cosmo asked as he dropped his own particularly large hairball into the bucket.

'I *could* – but I don't think I'd better . . .' Meowface said, keeping one eye on a particularly large and angry-looking ginger tom who had also arrived without a hairball and who was now scowling at Meowface from his perch on top of one of the sinks. 'I'll ask Cleo what to do later, but for now I can't let any cat inside unless they have the entry fee. Sorry.'

'I'll wait with you then, Mia,' Cosmo offered.

'Oh no,' Mia mewed back quickly. 'I'd hate *you* to miss the competition too. Besides, if you win that toy mouse, we can *both* play with it!'

So Cosmo reluctantly set off on his own after the others.

The assembly hall soon filled up with cats, all of whom had spent the last twenty-four hours grooming themselves and practising how to walk up and down as elegantly as possible. In the end there were nearly a hundred cats inside the hall, as well as eleven (including Mia) who had turned up without hairballs. Each of the eleven cats promised that they would deliver their entry fee by the end of the competition and so, after conferring with the other judges, Cleo instructed Meowface to let them in too.

Cosmo was thrilled that Mia now had the chance to be in the competition, and the two kittens purred excitedly as they stood side by side listening to Cleo telling everybody what was going to happen next.

'This is how we are going to conduct the auditions today,' Cleo announced in his most actorish voice. 'The judges' task is to choose the cats who will be the contestants in my catwalk show tomorrow. So what we want *you* to do is walk around the hall, imagining that you are on a catwalk. While you are doing this, we will come round and choose which cats we think might have the F factor. If you feel a paw tapping you on the shoulder, that means we have chosen you as a finalist. Now—' he gave his most dramatic pause yet, actually stopping to chew one of his claws before finally miaowing out the words every cat in the room was waiting for – '*Let the auditions begin!*'

Cosmo and Mia did their best to walk around the hall as elegantly as possible, but it was difficult because they kept bumping into other cats who were all trying to do the same. At the far end of the hall a cat fight soon started up between three female alley cats and a pedigree tom who had collided into each other in a most inelegant fashion at the same moment that Cleo Cattrap had happened to be looking in their direction.

Cosmo noticed his father whispering something in Felina's ear and then the two judges started to walk towards their two kittens. Suddenly Cosmo realized something. 'It's not very fair that our parents are the judges, is it?' he whispered to Mia. 'I mean, they're bound to pick us instead of the other kittens.'

But Mephisto and Felina had obviously thought about that too. 'We are going to leave the kitten section of the competition for Cleo Cattrap to judge alone,' Mephisto told them. 'Cosmo, you are easily the most handsome kitten in the room, which is no wonder considering that your mother and I are such fine-looking cats. However, it would not be fair if I picked you.'

'Or if I picked *you*, Mia,' Felina added.

'Just make sure you look as sleek and well-groomed as possible at all times,' Mephisto

127

reminded Cosmo. 'And don't scratch your-self when Cleo is watching.'

When they were out of earshot, Cosmo turned to Mia. 'Being in a catwalk competition is much harder work than I thought it would be.'

'I know,' Mia agreed. 'But we can't give up now. Look, Cleo's heading this way. Let's try and look as elegant as *he* does.'

And both kittens began to swing their bottoms in an exaggerated manner and take dainty steps as they walked, while lifting their chins as high up in the air as they would go.

8

That evening, Cosmo and his parents were celebrating. Cosmo had been picked as one of the ten kitten finalists, and so had Mia and Hagnus. Unfortunately Matty had ruined her chances by sitting down with her hind leg in the air to wash a bit of fur she thought she had missed that morning, which was probably the least elegant posture she could have adopted just as Cleo happened to be passing.

Ten adult finalists had also been chosen including, much to Cleo's horror, a female Persian with the most perfectly short nose he had ever seen.

A huge row had started up when Mephisto had invited the white Persian, who he had met in the street, to enter the competition at the last minute. Cleo had tried to say that the auditions were now closed, but then the Persian cat had produced the largest hairball out of all that had been donated so far, and he had been persuaded to let her in. But he had had no intention of letting her be in the final.

Cleo had therefore been furious when Mephisto and Felina had *both* chosen the Persian as one of their final ten, and he had found himself outvoted. He had been so angry that he had refused to go home with Mephisto and Cosmo after the auditions, and he had stayed on at the school instead, saying he would sleep there for the night.

Needless to say, Mephisto hadn't minded losing his house-guest one bit, and he was looking quite smug as he gazed down on Cosmo with half-closed eyes from the seat of his favourite armchair.

131

'If I win that toy mouse,' Cosmo was telling him excitedly, 'I'm going to share it with Mia, and if she wins she's going to share it with me.'

'You'll soon have nine younger kittens to share your toys with,' India pointed out as she heaved herself up on to the sofa. 'I hope you're going to play gently with them, Cosmo. They'll be a lot smaller than you to start with.'

Cosmo tried to imagine what it would be like to have nine little brothers and sisters. 'Nine is quite a lot, isn't it?' he said.

Mephisto had clearly been thinking that too. 'Is it possible Felina might have got it wrong?' he asked India as he eyed her tummy.

Just then they heard the cat flap opening and the professor-cat calling out to them from the kitchen.

'I don't think that's likely, do you?' India murmured, looking amused as she added, 'But you can ask her if you want.'

Mephisto licked his paw and didn't reply.

'Is it all right if Mia and I come in and eat some of your Crunchies munchies?' Felina asked as she came into the living room. 'All Amy's given us is that anti-hairball cat food again.'

Mia *still* hadn't produced a hairball – and she was under strict instructions from Cleo to deliver one by tomorrow or she'd be disqualified from the competition.

'Eat as much as you want,' India told her.

As it happened, Cosmo's household had plenty of food. Not only had the Two-Shoes family left them a whole pile of dried stuff, but Mephisto had also brought them some fresh fish he had smelt in a kitchen on his way home. (Humans often left their back

133

doors and kitchen windows open when they'd been cooking fish, which Mephisto always took as an invitation to help himself.) Mephisto, India and Cosmo had therefore eaten well that evening, and there had even been a small piece of fish left over which India had suggested they save in case one of them got peckish during the night.

Cosmo was worried that Mia wouldn't produce a hairball by the next day, despite changing her diet, and now he had a very good idea.

He didn't tell the others what he was thinking because Mia was there and he didn't want to get her hopes up. But while the other cats were talking he went to find the leftover fish that his mother had put away behind the dustbin, and picked it up carefully between his jaws. It smelt very tasty and Cosmo couldn't imagine how Cleo could resist it.

Cosmo slipped out through the cat flap without the others noticing, and when he got to the school he jumped in through the toilet window and found Cleo standing in front of two piles of hairballs, holding something long and black between his teeth.

Cosmo's tail immediately bushed up and he dropped the fish.

'Where did you get that?' he mewed in alarm. The thing Cleo was holding was a witch's wand.

Cleo, who wasn't a witch-cat and had therefore never seen a witch's wand before, dropped it on to the floor to reply. 'This is the flea detector I told you about. I've just used it to test these hairballs – and far too many of them have got fleas inside!' He let out a very angry yowl.

'But that's a witch's wand,' Cosmo told him quickly, coming over to join him. 'It looks like it's been programmed with a spell. Who gave it to you?'

Cleo stopped yowling and rubbed his nose with his paw. 'That witch I went to see, of course. I'm not allowed to tell you her name. She needs me to give her a hundred hairballs, but she won't accept them unless they're flea-less, which is why she

136

gave me this flea detector to test them with. She said all I had to do was wave it over each hairball in turn and it would beep if there was a flea inside. She said any hairball with a flea had to be thrown away. And since sixteen of these hairballs have fleas inside, that means I'm nowhere near my target number.'

Cosmo was sniffing the wand now. 'It must have been programmed with a flea-detecting spell,' he told Cleo. 'But why does this witch of yours want a hundred hairballs? What's she going to do with them?' Cosmo knew that cat hairballs could be used as ingredients in witches' spells, but he also knew that they weren't rare enough or powerful enough to be very valuable.

'How should *I* know?' Cleo replied, looking cross. 'I don't care about that! What matters to *me* is what she's promised me in return!'

'What *has* she promised you?' Cosmo asked curiously.

Cleo shook his head as if he couldn't possibly tell, then he started to recount the hairballs, which he had just divided into two piles – the ones that didn't have fleas in them, and the ones that did.

'Cleo, please tell me,' Cosmo urged. 'Maybe I can help you!'

'How could a little kitten like you help *me*?' Cleo scoffed.

'Because I'm a witch-cat, and witch-cats aren't like ordinary cats! We have magic sneezes that are quite powerful.'

'Powerful enough to remove fleas from hairballs?' Cleo looked more interested now.

'Maybe,' Cosmo said. 'But first you've got

to tell me *why* you need these hairballs so much.'

Cleo lowered his head and avoided meeting Cosmo's eyes. Then he seemed to come to a decision and he looked up again. 'If I tell you, you mustn't tell anyone else,' he said. 'This has to be *our* secret, you understand?'

'Of course,' Cosmo agreed.

So Cleo jumped up on to the nearest sink, where he stood and stared at himself in the mirror for a few moments. Then he looked down at Cosmo and began to tell him the story of his life – about how he had never felt good enough compared to other Persian cats because his nose wasn't as short as it should be. 'This witch has offered to perform a spell on my nose that will make it as short as any other Persian's,' Cleo finished. 'She'll do it for me in exchange for a hundred hairballs. But now I haven't got a

139

hundred to give her!' He started to yowl again, only this time it was a true yowl of despair.

Cosmo felt so sorry for Cleo that he went to fetch the piece of fish he had brought with him and dropped it on the floor in front of the older cat, hoping it might cheer him up. It did, but only for the twenty seconds it took Cleo to eat it. Then he started to yowl unhappily again.

'Cleo, *I* think your face is nice just how it is,' Cosmo tried to reassure him. 'So does Mother. *I* think cats with flat faces look silly, even if they *are* pedigree Persians.'

'Mephisto and Felina don't think that though, do they?' Cleo said. 'They've just picked a pure-bred Persian to be in my Catwalk final! Oh, I should never have let your mother convince me to share the judging. My career will be ruined now – and it's the only thing I have!' And he started to yowl again quite hysterically.

'Cleo, please stop making that noise,' Cosmo begged him. 'I think I know how to get rid of these fleas.' Cosmo was remembering something he had seen his father do once, when Goody had been making a spell and had accidently emptied a whole jar of human dandruff into her cauldron, instead of the sprinkling of it that the spell required.

Cleo stopped in mid-yowl, and stared at Cosmo. 'You do?'

'I *think* so.' Cosmo quickly selected one of the sixteen hairballs that had a flea in it and nudged it across the floor so that it was apart from the others. Then he started to search the surrounding area for something that would make him sneeze.

It was quite dusty in one corner so he stuck his nose into the dust and breathed in. Soon his nose felt very ticklish inside.

'Right,' he told Cleo. 'I'm ready.' He knew that he had to produce exactly the same sort of sneeze he had seen his father do on the day Goody had had her dandruff problem.

As Cleo watched anxiously, Cosmo turned his back on the hairball, then twisted his head round to sneeze backwards over his left shoulder. And as he sneezed, he thought as hard as he could about fleas. As the sneeze droplets showered down over the hairball, it began to glow, almost as if it had been lit up from the inside.

'I've just done a removing spell on it,' Cosmo explained to Cleo. 'It's meant to remove the thing you're thinking about when you sneeze. But it's the first time I've ever done one, so I hope it's worked.'

'Let's use the flea detector and see.' Cleo anxiously picked up the wand between his teeth and held the tip of it over the hairball. This time it didn't beep! Cleo dropped the wand and started to race around the room in a way he hadn't done since he was a young kitten. 'We've done it!' he miaowed loudly. 'Another fifteen sneezes and I'll have all the hairballs I need!'

'One sneeze will easily cover several hairballs,' Cosmo said hastily. 'Let's divide them up into batches of five, shall we? Then I'll only have to do three more sneezes.'

And so, three magic sneezes later, all the hairballs were flea-free.

143

Cleo had managed to collect ninety-nine hairballs that day, including the particularly large (and thankfully flea-less) specimen he had contributed himself, so now all he needed was a final one to make up his total.

'Remember the eleven cats I let into my auditions without their entry fees?' he said to Cosmo. 'Well, not one of them gave me a hairball afterwards like they promised. And since only one adult and one kitten among them have been picked as finalists, they're the only two I can expect to get hairballs from now. The kitten is your friend Mia, of course.'

'I was going to ask you about Mia,' Cosmo said, suddenly remembering why he had come to see Cleo in the first place. 'I was wondering if that fish I gave you could be her entry-fee *instead* of a hairball?'

'But I need her hairball,' Cleo said. 'I'm depending on her. What if that other cat doesn't give me one?'

'Yes, but she's having trouble bringing one up . . . it's not her fault . . . she's really trying . . . and since I've just done you this special favour . . .'

'Which I'm very grateful for, Cosmo,' Cleo put in quickly. 'But we can't have the other contestants thinking I'm showing favouritism towards Mia because her mother is one of the judges, can we? You know how cross cats can get if they think they're being cheated out of anything.'

'Well couldn't you just *say* that Mia's given you a hairball?' Cosmo suggested, a little uncertainly now.

'You want me to *lie*?' Cleo looked horrified. 'Can you imagine what would happen if it ever leaked out that I had been dishonest, Cosmo? No cat would take *Cleo Cattrap's Amazing Catwalk Extravaganza* seriously ever again! Besides, don't you see? All our hard work tonight . . . all *your* hard work . . . won't count for anything if I don't get my last hairball. And Mia and that other cat are my only chance.'

'It's just that I don't know if Mia is going to be *able* to bring up a hairball in time—' Cosmo began in a small voice.

'Don't you worry about that,' Cleo swiftly reassured him. 'I will give Mia all day tomorrow to produce her hairball – and she can chew all the grass in the school grounds if she likes, to help her. Now . . . hadn't you better be going home?'

'I suppose,' Cosmo said.

Cleo purred loudly. 'Sleep well tonight, my little hero. *I* will – thanks to you!' And he gave Cosmo an appreciative lick on top of his head, before starting to make himself comfortable on top of his collection of hair-balls, which he judged would make a nice soft surface on which to curl up.

'I wouldn't lie there if I were you,' Cosmo warned him as he jumped up to exit through the window.

'Why not?' Cleo stood up in alarm. 'Is there some magic left in them that might harm me?'

'No, but you don't want to give them more fleas, do you?'

And before Cleo could tell him off for being cheeky – and point out that the great Cleo Cattrap had never had a flea in his life – Cosmo had disappeared outside.

147

9

Cosmo got back to find that Felina and Mia had gone home, but that Scarlett and Bunty had just arrived, having come to check on the cats and to refill their food and water bowls. Bunty had also come to look for a

spell recipe which she had previously lent to Goody.

'It's a recipe for a special potion that stops bad spells coming down your chimney,' Bunty explained. 'Since there are so many chimneys in the Witch Hospital I think it's worth putting a spell-block on them while the babies are so vulnerable.'

'How *are* the babies?' India wanted to know. (India found that she had become particularly concerned about babies of all species since she had become pregnant – to her amazement she *even* felt quite benignly towards puppies.)

'They're all fine, thank goodness,' Bunty told her. 'None of them seem any the worse for having their toenails clipped.'

'But they aren't allowed to leave the hospital until their toenails have grown back a bit,' Scarlett added. 'Dad's going to stay

149

there with Spike and Mum until then, just in case that fake midwife turns up again.'

'India, you seem to have put on an awful lot of weight recently,' Bunty said suddenly, as India started to make her way towards the newly replenished water bowl. Her large belly was almost touching the floor as she walked.

India gave a polite, non-committal mew. She didn't want any two-legged interference when she delivered her kittens, and she was therefore keeping as quiet as possible about her condition.

Fortunately Bunty's attention was immediately caught by Mephisto, who was scratching himself very vigorously behind one ear. 'I hope you haven't got fleas, Mephisto,' she said, frowning.

As Scarlett went upstairs to collect some things from her bedroom, Cosmo bounded

after her. As she reached the upstairs land-ing, Scarlett saw something odd fly past the window. It was an empty broomstick.

'Broomsticks don't usually fly about on their own, do they?' Scarlett said, going over to the window to look out.

'Not unless someone's put a spell on them,' Cosmo mewed.

Scarlett hurried back downstairs and out

through the front door where her own broomstick was lying beside Bunty's on the front lawn. From the garden she could still make out the empty broomstick in the sky, glowing at the back end where it had been powered up by magic.

Cosmo, who had followed her downstairs, noticed that their garage door was open and quickly went to look inside. Sybil's broomstick, which had been kept in a corner of the garage until now, was missing. As Scarlett joined him, she spotted that too.

'Come on, Cosmo!' she called, running back out into the garden again. 'Someone's put a spell on Sybil's broom! Let's follow it and see where it goes!'

It wasn't yet completely dark, but it would be soon. Sybil's broomstick was a long way ahead of theirs, still glowing at the end, and they had to fly very fast to catch up with it. It led them over endless rooftops — human ones with ordinary chimneys and witch ones with pink chimneys — and over the park and the railway line before it stopped abruptly and began to descend.

They finally saw it fly down the chimney of a witch's cottage that was situated at the end of a long twisty road. The cottage was set back from the road, well away from all the other houses in the street, which, judging from their chimneys, all belonged to humans. As Scarlett and Cosmo flew closer to the house they saw a green plaque on its front gate that said *Sticky-End Cottage*.

'I hope it's not called that because anyone who visits here comes to a sticky end,' Cosmo mewed nervously.

'I wonder who lives here,' Scarlett murmured as she flew her own broomstick twice

153

around the cottage, which had a pink chimney that was billowing out green smoke – a sure sign that the witch who lived there was home and that her cauldron was busy. But as all the curtains in the house were closed, it was impossible to see inside.

'This has got to be the perfect location for a bad witch's house,' Scarlett said. 'No close neighbours to get in your way when you're making evil spells, and only local humans to fool rather than other witches. We'd better get back and tell Aunt Bunty.' She noted the name of the street – *Rattlesnake Road* – before heading home.

Back at the house, Bunty was in the kitchen brewing up her chimney-blocking spell in the family cauldron, and Mephisto was out in the garden looking for Cosmo. As Scarlett's broomstick landed on the grass, Mephisto called out crossly for his kitten to

155

come inside at once. This particular spell of Bunty's needed two magic sneezes from two different witch-cats, so Mephisto and Cosmo were both required to help.

Scarlett and her aunt stood back to watch as the two witch-cats climbed up the cat steps on either side of the cauldron, and sneezed into it at exactly the same time. 'A-A-A-TISHOO!' Their sneeze droplets

immediately reacted with the other spell ingredients, and the liquid inside the cauldron began to bubble ferociously. Soon red and white stars began to shoot out of it.

'When it's settled down a bit, I'll bottle some up and take it to the hospital,' Bunty told them.

Scarlett started to tell her aunt about Sybil's broomstick flying off on its own, and how she and Cosmo had followed it.

Bunty frowned. 'You should have come to tell me before you flew off all by yourself like that, Scarlett! A witch-child and a witch-kitten are no match for a truly bad adult witch. You know that very well!'

'Sorry, Aunt Bunty,' Scarlett said quickly, 'but don't you want to know where we ended up?'

After Scarlett had told her everything, Bunty said, 'The Broom sisters used to live

157

at the end cottage in Rattlesnake Road. It was put up for sale when they were both sent to prison. I don't know who bought it after that.'

'It's called *Sticky*-End Cottage now,' Scarlett said.

'Well, first thing tomorrow I'll ask the Good Witches' Society to find out who lives there.'

After the two witches had gone, Mephisto told Cosmo it was time he got some rest. India had already curled up for the night on top of Goody and Gabriel's bed, and Mephisto told Cosmo to go upstairs and join her. 'You've got a big day ahead tomorrow,' Mephisto reminded his kitten, 'and you *should* be trying to get as much sleep as possible – not racing around after stray broomsticks.'

'Yes, Father,' Cosmo replied meekly. He was always being told by his parents that sleep was very important, and that every cat must try and fit as much of it as possible into its daily routine. The trouble was, Cosmo thought as he bounded upstairs, a lot of the time life was so exciting that you couldn't help wanting to stay awake.

At Sticky-End Cottage the telephone was ringing. Selina Slaughter, who had lived there since the Broom sisters had been forced to move out, hurried to answer it. She was feeling grumpy because she had just given her white mice some Stilton cheese for their supper as a special treat and they had rather ungratefully left it untouched, saying that they preferred cheddar.

'You're lucky I feed you anything at all!' she shouted at them as she went to answer

159

the phone. 'One of these days I'm going to feed *you* as supper to the local cats! Do you think *they'll* complain? *Oh, Selina, I'm afraid we don't really like white mice – we only eat grey ones.* I don't think so!'

She picked up the phone and found that the person at the other end was Murdina Broom.

'We're only allowed one phone call a week, so Sybil's asked me to ring you on her behalf,' Murdina said, keeping her voice low. 'She wants to know if you managed to recover her broomstick?'

'Of course I have – it's just arrived,' Selina replied, feeling a little irritated at being checked up on.

'Excellent. Well, *I'm* going to need a broom as well, and since there should be a couple of spare ones kicking about in the basement of my cottage I was wondering if—'

'Don't you mean *my* cottage?' Selina interrupted her coldly.

'What? Oh, yes, yes . . . of course . . . I keep forgetting . . . anyway, if you could bring me one too I'd be most grateful.' Murdina dropped her voice even further as she added, 'Sybil also wants to let you know that the Great Escape must take place tomorrow!'

'*Tomorrow?*'

'Yes. Tomorrow is community-service day. She says we can't wait another week until the next one – the magic in the toenails might have worn off by then.'

'But I haven't collected the hairballs yet!'

'Well, surely you can do that tomorrow morning. And one more thing . . . Sybil thinks that we ought to provide some sort of *extra* distraction for that interfering

161

Two-Shoes family, just to make sure they stay out of our way. We've already agreed to send a nasty spell in the direction of baby Spike – but Sybil's just had another idea. She says that the Two-Shoes family have a daughter and she thinks it might be a good idea to kidnap her. Sybil knows you're busy, but she was wondering if she could trouble you to arrange that as well.'

Selina quickly assured Murdina that kidnapping Scarlett Two-Shoes would be no trouble at all. 'On the contrary, it will be an absolute pleasure!' she said, smiling at the thought of it.

And the two witches had a very pleasant cackle together until Murdina's phone credit ran out and she was obliged to hang up.

The following morning, the ten kittens and ten adult cats who had been chosen as catwalk finalists were all waiting in the school assembly hall for the judges to appear. Neither Mia nor the adult cat who still owed its entry fee had managed to produce a hairball yet, though the adult – a handsome black cat with a white moustache who went by the name of Albert-of-the-street – swore that he could feel one sitting in his tummy. 'I'm sure I'll have it out by lunchtime at the latest,' he told the others confidently.

'You'd better or you'll be disqualified from the competition,' piped up a fluffy grey kitten (who might have had a bit of Persian in him, but certainly not a lot). 'And so will you, Mia!' the kitten added, looking quite pleased at the prospect of losing one of his rivals.

The adult Persian, whose name was Tallulah Poppypuss, was standing a little apart from the others, licking her front

163

paws. 'This competition is not just about winning, you know,' she said in a very silky voice. 'It's a celebration of feline-ness!'

'Yeah . . . right . . .' Albert-of-the-street replied, looking as if he thought the Persian was totally dippy.

The cats all fell silent as the three judges and Meowface entered the room.

'Welcome to Cleo Cattrap's Catwalk Finals,' Cleo announced grandly, walking around the group of cats as he spoke.

Cosmo noticed that he avoided looking at Tallulah, whose big blue eyes seemed full of admiration for him.

'First we will have a rehearsal, so that you all know how to behave on the catwalk,' Cleo told them. 'The kittens will rehearse first, then they can go off and play while I spend the rest of the morning with the adults. The competition itself will start at midday. Meowface has been telling all the neighbouring cats about it, so we are expecting a large audience.'

For the next hour Cosmo and the other kittens practised how to walk along the catwalk bench in as elegant a manner as possible – and how to pause dramatically at the end and lift one paw fetchingly off the ground, posing like that for several seconds in front of the audience. 'You must keep your faces very serious-looking the whole time,' Cleo told them. 'No grinning is allowed, and any cat who gets a bushy tail will be disqualified.'

'And no *chasing* your tails – or anybody else's,' Felina added, looking sternly at her daughter.

Hagnus was already so excited that the fur on his tail was starting to stand on end, and now he had to lick it furiously to get it to stay flat. Matty, who was watching from the side, rushed over to help him.

After the kittens had finished rehearsing, Meowface told Cosmo that his mother was waiting to speak to him. Apparently she was feeling too heavy to jump through the toilet window today, and she wanted him to meet her outside instead.

India told Cosmo that Scarlett had just called at the house. 'Bunty wanted her to take me to see the vet, would you believe?' India miaowed indignantly. 'Apparently it's suddenly occurred to her that I might be pregnant. Well, if she thinks she's getting me anywhere near that dreadful-smelling vet with all his needles and his waiting room full of nasty yapping dogs, she's quite wrong. Fortunately I managed to escape through the cat flap while the child was off hunting for the cat-carrier.' India paused to lick her tummy protectively before continuing. 'But Scarlett had something she wanted to tell *you*, Cosmo. She kept rambling on about some cottage you'd been to together, and how she'd found out something important about the witch who lives there.'

Cosmo's ears pricked up. 'I'd better go and speak to her,' he said. 'Mother, will you tell Meowface I'll be back in time for the competition, but that I've got something I need to do first?' And he quickly raced off towards home.

*

By the time Cosmo got back to the house, Scarlett had gone. Two kitchen chairs were turned over and so was the rubbish bin, and Cosmo could only assume that India had had to make more of an effort to escape from Scarlett than she'd let on. Feeling slightly puzzled, Cosmo borrowed Goody's broomstick and headed for Bunty's house.

He arrived there just as Bunty was coming out through her front door. 'Is Scarlett with you?' he asked her.

'No, Cosmo. Actually she's taken your mother to see the vet – just for a check-up you understand. There's nothing to worry about.'

'It's just that Scarlett said she had something she wanted to tell me,' Cosmo mewed, deciding it was best not to mention that his mother had skipped her appointment and that Scarlett was probably out looking for her right now.

'Oh, well *I* can tell you what that was, Cosmo,' Bunty replied. 'This morning we found out that the witch who lives in Sticky-End Cottage is called Selina Slaughter. We put her name into the Witch Computer and

169

when her picture came up on the screen, Scarlett recognized her as the fake midwife who stole Spike's toenails. Two of my colleagues from the Good Witches' Society have just gone to her cottage to question her. Apparently she's got a criminal record and she's known to be an old crony of Sybil's. I'm on my way to the prison now, to ask Sybil what *she* knows about all this.' Bunty paused. 'Actually, it might help if you came too, Cosmo. You know Sybil better than I do and you might be able to tell better than I can whether she's lying or not. If I promise not to leave you alone with her and I let you sit on my lap the whole time, will you come with me?'

Cosmo bravely agreed, but he couldn't stop the tight feeling at the back of his throat from turning into a very uneasy growl at the prospect of coming face to face with Sybil again.

10

At the Witch Prison there was quite a party atmosphere evident in the communal kitchens, where some of the prisoners were helping to prepare the lunch. None of them usually enjoyed community-service day, because doing good deeds instead of bad ones made most of them feel quite squeamish, but today was different. Today was the day they had all been waiting for. In just a few hours time, as long as nothing went wrong with Sybil's Great Escape plan, one hundred of them would be free. And so every witch was very excited.

'This community won't know what's hit it when I get out of here,' Murdina Broom was saying – and all the other witches cackled with laughter as they thought about their

171

own plans to take revenge on the community that had imprisoned them.

Sybil was in the middle of mixing up a large bowl of lumpy custard when one of the prison guards came to tell her that she had a visitor – Bunty Two-Shoes.

'I don't want to see *her*,' Sybil protested vehemently, but the guard told her she had no choice.

Fortunately Murdina Broom managed to whisper some words of warning in Sybil's ear. 'Stay calm, Sybil. You don't want them to suspect anything is wrong.'

Sybil managed to compose herself before entering the visiting room, so much so that she shocked Bunty by smiling at her quite warmly. (She had a very good pretend smile which she had been working on ever since she'd been in prison.) She even managed to stay calm when she saw Cosmo, though her

mouth turned down at both ends for a second or two, before she extended her hand
towards him.

Cosmo hissed at her.

'Dear Cosmo,' she said as she snatched
her hand back, 'I was only going to stroke
you. There's no need for you to be afraid.
Why, I've been completely rehabilitated here
in prison. I've seen the error of my ways and

I'm quite reformed.' She let out a laugh that was almost a cackle, but not quite.

Cosmo didn't believe her. Sybil seemed exactly the same to him as when he'd last seen her – apart from the red ear-tag she wore, which looked a bit like an earring but that Cosmo knew was her prison security tag.

'Don't worry, Cosmo,' Bunty said. 'I won't let her hurt you.'

'*Shame!*' Sybil hissed, then added quickly, 'Shame the poor little dear thinks I'd want to hurt him, I mean!'

'Sybil, we've come to ask you about your friend Selina Slaughter,' Bunty said.

'Oh, but I haven't been friends with her for years!'

'Then why has she visited you every week since you've been in prison?' (Bunty had asked to see the prison visitors' book on her

174

arrival and had noted that Selina had been Sybil's only visitor.)

'Oh, she has *visited* me, yes,' Sybil quickly agreed. 'But I would hardly call her a friend. I would say she is more a . . . well . . . a *role model*. You see, Selina was once a bad witch too. That's why she's been visiting me − to teach me how to become a good witch instead of a bad one. Only a good witch who has once been very bad herself can help someone like me, you see.' Sybil placed both her palms together under her chin in an attempt to look angelic.

Bunty glared at her. 'Your broomstick was observed entering Selina's chimney last night. Did you give her permission to take it?'

'Permission? Now, let me think . . . I might have mentioned that my broomstick was at my old house . . . just in passing. But

175

Selina couldn't have stolen it. Selina is as honest as the day is short . . . or should I say *long*?' Sybil gave a sly smile.

'Someone who is certainly *not* honest has just organized the stealing of a great many witch-babies' toenails,' Bunty said sharply.

Sybil looked shocked. 'I don't believe it! Who would steal the toenails from poor little darling witch-babies? How dreadful!'

'Yes,' Bunty said. 'It *is* dreadful. And we know for a fact that your friend Selina is involved. My niece, Scarlett, has already identified her as the midwife who stole my baby nephew's toenails just a few days ago.'

'Ah, but then it can't be Selina! Selina isn't a midwife. Oh no! The very idea of it! Selina doesn't even *like* babies! She'd certainly never do a job where she was helping them to get *born*!' Sybil burst out laughing, as if she had just made a hilarious joke.

'Sybil, do you know of any reason why Selina would want to steal witch-babies' toenails?' Bunty asked her sternly. 'And remember . . . if we find out later that you've been hiding something from us, you'll be punished too.'

'You don't mean I'll have to spend even *more* time in prison, do you?' Sybil said. 'Because the strange thing is, I'm beginning to rather like it here! I've made *so* many new friends and I just *love* doing my community service. I never realized that helping old ladies to cross the road could be so much fun. And as for working at the flea clinic and getting rid of those pesky cats . . . sorry . . . I mean pesky *fleas* from those *dear* little cats . . . that is most rewarding also.' She beamed at Cosmo. 'Have you any fleas you'd like me to squeeze out for you while you're here, my dear? I've grown my fingernails

177

nice and sharp so I'm very good at digging out the little pests. It's a little painful for the cats, I'm told – but no worse than being at the vet! And you know what they say – no pain, no gain!'

'Sybil, you have been most unhelpful, just as I expected,' Bunty told her coldly. 'But we'll be keeping an eye on you – and we *will* find out the truth!'

'Oh, I doubt *that*,' Sybil murmured, but so quietly that only Cosmo heard her, because cat-hearing is extra sharp.

As soon as they had left the prison, Bunty used her mobile phone to call the chair-woman of the Good Witches' Society, who told her that her two colleagues had failed to find Selina at her house.

'She'll show up sooner or later,' Bunty said as she put her phone back in her handbag. 'And then we'll get to the bottom of all this.

I'd better go up to the hospital and tell Goody and Gabriel what's been happening. Do you want to come, Cosmo? Scarlett might be there by now.'

'I have to go somewhere else,' Cosmo said. 'But tell Scarlett I'll see her later!'

Cosmo arrived back at the school just in time for the kittens' catwalk competition. The kittens were all gathered in the toilets giving themselves final preparatory licks, and the audience of cats in the assembly hall was making a loud din as it got ready to watch the show.

'Where's Mia?' Cosmo asked Hagnus, seeing that she wasn't with the others.

'I haven't seen her since rehearsals,' Hagnus replied. 'I thought she must be with you.'

Felina suddenly appeared, also looking for

179

Mia. 'Cleo says it's time for you to go through now,' she told the kittens.

'Mia hasn't been disqualified from the competition for not producing a hairball, has she?' Cosmo asked, thinking that if that was the case Mia might well have gone home in a huff.

'No,' Felina replied. 'Mia and Albert-of-the-street were both told that they could be in the competition, so long as one of them gave Cleo a hairball before they went home today. Come to think of it, I haven't seen Albert-of-the-street recently either.'

And suddenly Cosmo didn't care about the catwalk competition any more. He had a feeling that he couldn't explain – a feeling that made him shiver all down his spine.

'We'd better start looking for them,' he told Felina. 'You search inside the building and I'll search outside.'

'But you'll miss the contest,' Felina said in surprise.

'That doesn't matter. I just want to find Mia.'

Half an hour later when Cosmo and Felina met up again in the assembly hall, the kitten competition was over. The grey fluffy kitten had been chosen as the winner. Cleo had had a tear in his eye as he'd announced that the grey kitten reminded him of himself at that age – which was the reason he had awarded him first place.

Cosmo hurried over to Mephisto. 'Father, we can't find Mia *anywhere*! I'm worried something's happened to her.'

'Albert-of-the-street is missing too,' Felina added.

'How odd. Do you think the two of them could have gone off somewhere together?' Mephisto suggested.

181

'Mia would never go off with a cat she hardly knows!' Felina hissed crossly. (She was very upset about losing her kitten, and when she was upset she always got extremely hissy.)

'Now, now . . . there's nothing to be alarmed about,' Cleo said, looking a little flustered. 'I can tell you exactly where they are. You see, my witch friend arrived earlier to collect her hairballs, and when I told her I was one short she got rather cross with me. So I explained that two cats still *owed* me hairballs and she said that she would . . . err . . . well . . . *borrow* those two cats until they had produced them. She assured me they would get a very nice tea if they went with her to her cottage. So I sent them outside where she was waiting for them. She must have persuaded them to go with her, I suppose.'

182

'*Persuaded* them?' Felina hissed.

'Cleo, how could you be so stupid?' Mephisto spat out.

'Cleo, you've got to tell us the name of this witch – and where she lives!' Cosmo mewed.

'But I can't! I promised I—' Cleo broke off abruptly, backing away from the other cats. 'Her name is Selina Slaughter,' he mumbled. 'But I'm sure she wouldn't hurt a fly. Why, she makes such *delicious* tuna sandwiches!'

'Selina Slaughter lives at Sticky-End Cottage and she's the same witch who stole Spike's toenails,' Cosmo told them. 'Bunty's been trying to find her too. She's a friend of Sybil's!'

Mephisto's tail bushed up and he growled deep in his throat. 'Any friend of Sybil's is an enemy of ours! We must go after Mia at once!'

11

'I think a few of us need to sneak into this cottage and rescue Mia quietly before Selina finds out we're on to her,' Tani said. 'We don't want her flying into a panic. A bad witch in a panic is always a dangerous thing.'

'I agree with you,' Mephisto said. 'As the most senior witch-cat here, I will head up the rescue party. Cosmo – you must come too and show us the way.'

'I'm coming as well,' Felina said firmly. 'I know I'm not a witch-cat, but Mia is my kitten.'

And so it was decided that Mephisto, Tani, Cosmo and Felina would all fly to Sticky-End Cottage on Goody's broomstick. Felina had never ridden a broomstick before and she was a little nervous at the

185

prospect, but Cosmo quickly reassured her. 'Don't worry – you can sit in the basket. Mia always sits in the basket whenever I take *her* flying and she says it's very comfortable. She says—' He broke off as it suddenly hit him that unless they found Mia soon, she wouldn't be going broomstick-riding with him ever again.

The rescue party (with Tani's two kittens in tow) quickly set off for Cosmo's house. As Cosmo went to find a suitably large basket to hook over the end of the broom, Matty and Hagnus were told by their mother to stay there with India, who was upstairs having a rest.

'I don't see why *we* can't be part of the rescue party too,' Hagnus protested in his whiniest miaow. 'It's not fair that you're letting Cosmo go and not us!'

'Cosmo is the only one who knows the

186

way to the witch's cottage,' Tani told him firmly.

'*Cleo* knows it too!' Hagnus pointed out stubbornly.

'Cleo Cattrap is not to be trusted!' Mephisto growled, so fiercely that Hagnus decided to drop his argument and do as he was told instead.

With Mephisto in control of their broom speed, it didn't take them long to reach Rattlesnake Road,

at which point they slowed down and took care not to draw attention to themselves as they approached Selina's cottage.

'Bunty said that the Broom sisters used to live here, and I know they had a cat,' Mephisto said, 'which means there's bound to be a cat flap in the back door.'

They landed the broomstick behind a large bush, so that they wouldn't be spotted if Selina was looking out of the window. Then they crept towards the back door where the old cat flap was still in position.

'Follow me,' Mephisto whispered.

It was very quiet inside the kitchen and it seemed as if nobody was at home. A large cauldron was sitting in the fireplace, but there was nothing brewing inside it. 'She was definitely making a spell last night,' Cosmo said, 'because Scarlett and I saw the smoke.'

'Let's split up and search the rest of the house,' Mephisto suggested. 'Cosmo, you come with me.'

Cosmo and his father soon found themselves in the living room, which was a perfectly ordinary-looking room at the opposite end of the cottage to the kitchen, with a big fireplace in the middle of one wall. Something about the room was bothering Cosmo, though, and after a minute or two he realized what it was. 'There's only one chimney on the roof of this cottage and it's at the other end of the house,' he told his father. 'So this can't be a real fireplace, can it?'

Mephisto immediately went over to inspect the fireplace more closely. He stood up on his hind legs to have a sniff inside the chimney and hissed as he bumped his head.

'There's no upwards chimney,' he told

189

Cosmo. 'This is a reverse fireplace. The old witch I lived with when I was a kitten had one of these. There must be a downwards chimney instead.' He started to nudge at various bits of the fireplace with his nose, until he uncovered a loose piece of coal that was sparkling rather conspicuously, as if it contained magic. Mephisto prodded it with his paw and mewed at Cosmo to stand back.

Just in time Cosmo moved out of the way as the fireplace started to make a loud grinding noise.

Felina and Tani heard the noise and came to see what was happening. 'The rest of the house seems empty,' Tani said, 'apart from some white mice locked in a cage in one of the upstairs rooms. We offered to let them loose, but they shrieked at us to go away.' She let out a surprised mew as the fireplace started to swing upwards and outwards.

190

They all stared at it in amazement until it stopped moving, then Mephisto gingerly stepped forward to peer down into the hole that had been uncovered.

Almost immediately they heard a faint miaow coming from below.

'That's Mia!' Felina exclaimed.

'Come on,' Mephisto said. 'It won't be a big drop. Follow me.'

So they all jumped down into the chimney, which was obviously what Selina did herself when she wanted to descend, because a large soft cushion had been placed at the bottom on which to land.

They found themselves in a large underground cellar that was lit with green fluorescent lamps. There seemed to be a lot of bats hanging from the ceiling, though it was hard to tell if they were real, stuffed, or the artificial kind that many witches used to

191

decorate their houses. There was a big table in the centre of the room and in one corner was a large cage. Inside the cage sat Mia, Albert-of-the-street and – to everyone's surprise – Scarlett!

Cosmo rushed over and poked his nose between the bars to touch his two friends, and Felina went with him, clearly relieved to be reunited with her kitten again.

'I'm so glad you found us!' Scarlett gasped. 'Selina must have followed me home this morning. When I got back into the kitchen with the cat-carrier to take India to the vet, Selina was there waiting for me.'

Cosmo instantly remembered the signs of a struggle that he had seen in the kitchen earlier that day. It all made sense now.

Felina was licking Mia through the bars of the cage as Mia assured her mother that she hadn't been harmed – yet. 'But we have

193

to get out of here before Selina gets back!' she mewed.

'Stand back and I'll do a magic sneeze on the padlock,' Mephisto told them.

'I've already tried that,' Albert-of-the-street said gruffly. 'I'm a witch-cat too. She must have put some sort of anti-sneeze magic on the lock, because it doesn't work.'

'She said . . . she said if one of us hasn't brought up a hairball by the time she gets back, she'll take us to see Sybil at the flea clinic – and that Sybil will cut us open and help herself,' Mia told them in a frightened voice.

Felina growled fiercely and Scarlett said quickly, 'I think Selina will be back very soon. She's left a load of important spell ingredients on that table. She wouldn't tell me what spell she's making, but it definitely involves witch-babies' toenails.'

194

Cosmo, Mephisto and Tani all jumped up on to the table to look.

Cosmo gasped as he saw that all the hairballs Cleo had collected had been laid out in orderly rows. They looked like they were covered in little green spikes and, on closer inspection, it was clear that every hairball had ten green curly toenails wedged into it – each of which was glowing. The hairballs had been laid out in ten rows of ten (apart from the last row which only contained nine). They therefore totalled ninety-nine, with one extra set of toenails sitting on the table on its own.

Cosmo also spotted a piece of black paper with green spiky writing on it, which looked important. He lifted it up between his teeth and jumped down from the table to take it to Scarlett.

'This is a spell recipe,' Scarlett gasped as

195

soon as she saw it, and she started to read it out loud to them.

ANTI-TAGGING SPELL

This spell will allow you to remove stolen goods from shops because all electronic tags attached to the items will be deactivated. For each tag you will need the following:

1 cat hairball (any type of cat fur will do)

1 full set of newborn witch-baby toenail clippings (curled and glowing)

1 mouthful of witch saliva (one good spit should be ample)

VERY IMPORTANT: No fleas (dead or alive) must be left in the hairballs or this spell will not work!

Instructions: Simply press the toenail clippings into the hairball and then spit on it. The hairball can then be placed on to (or into) the item you wish to steal. Any electronic tag that is attached to the item will immediately cease to function.

Copyright © Murdina & Belinda Broom

When Scarlett had finished reading the spell, she said, 'Selina must be planning some really huge robbery! I wonder what it is that she's going to steal.'

'This must be the spell that the Broom sisters used to steal all those things from shops – the one that got them sent to prison,' Tani miaowed. 'Nobody ever knew exactly what they put in it along with the toenails, because the recipe itself was never found.'

197

'Murdina Broom is in prison with Sybil, isn't she?' Mephisto said. 'What if Murdina, Sybil and Selina are all planning another robbery together?'

'Selina has been visiting Sybil every week,' Cosmo told them. 'So they've definitely been plotting *something*.' He stopped to think some more, because a robbery just didn't seem the most likely thing somehow. After all, what pleasure could Sybil and Murdina get from stealing things like televisions that they couldn't actually use because they were locked up in prison? Unless . . .

'This spell works on electronic tags of *all* kinds, doesn't it?' Cosmo suddenly said.

The other cats looked at him, not sure what he was getting at.

'Sybil and all the other prisoners are *tagged* when they go outside the prison to do their community service, aren't they?' he continued slowly. 'So what if they're going to use this spell to de-tag *themselves*?'

'Of course!' Mephisto exclaimed, hissing with excitement at his kitten.

'*That's it, Cosmo!*' Tani gasped. 'Each witch will simply have to spit on a hairball with the toenails already inside, and she'll be de-tagged. Then she'll be able to escape – *without* being turned into a frog!'

'It's actually quite a brilliant idea,' Albert-of-the-street grunted.

'What day do the witches get let out of prison to do their community service?' Felina asked.

'Today!' Cosmo replied. 'When Bunty and I were at the prison this morning, they were getting ready to go out this afternoon.'

'Then they've got to be stopped!' Mephisto gave a loud growl as he switched into action-cat mode. 'Tani, you and Cosmo

199

had better go and raise the alarm. Felina and I will wait here in case Selina comes back.'

'What's going on?' Scarlett wanted to know, because she hadn't understood any of their excited mewing. Mia and Albert-of-the-street tried to make her understand by miaowing it all again very loudly, but she still couldn't follow what they were saying.

Tani and Cosmo hurried over to the chimney, meaning to climb back up into the main house again, but they soon found that the chimney wall was far too steep for them.

Mephisto went over to the chimney too, looking a bit sheepish all of a sudden. 'I've just recalled that when I lived with my first witch, she always had to carry me up the chimney in her arms,' he said. 'She had special boots with suckers on the front that helped *her* climb up. She was going to get

200

me some suckers for my paws, but she never got round to it.'

'Well, this is a fine time to tell us!' Felina burst out. 'Honestly, Mephisto, if you male cats would stop and *think* sometimes, before you went charging about all over the place!'

'It's not Mephisto's fault,' Tani said quickly. 'We were all in a rush to get to Mia when we heard her mew.'

Mephisto had already started to try and claw his way up the chimney himself, but even though he managed to get a little further than Tani and Cosmo, in the end his claws slipped and he slid down to the bottom.

Felina sighed. 'I suppose we'll just have to wait for Selina to come back, and pounce on her when she lands on the cushion,' she said. 'Maybe if we all bite and scratch her at once, we'll be able to make her do what we want.'

201

'I've got another idea,' Cosmo said, thinking about how he had unwittingly removed the fleas from sixteen hairballs the previous evening. 'Why don't we use our *own* fleas to stop the de-tagging spell from working?'

The adult cats looked at him in surprise.

'You know, this kid's pretty smart,' Albert-of-the-street said from inside the cage.

'Sometimes I think you are even smarter than Mother, Cosmo,' Mia gushed, gazing at her friend in total admiration.

'That's very clever thinking indeed, Cosmo,' his father agreed, giving his kitten a fond nip on the scruff of his neck. 'You're right! The more fleas we can find to put into these hairballs, the more witches we can stop escaping. The only problem is how are we going to do it?' It was notoriously difficult to remove a flea from your own fur just by scratching, and even though a lucky lick might remove one if you had a particularly flea-infested coat, licking was also far from efficient as a de-fleaing method.

The cats all turned to look at Scarlett. They were going to need her help to extract enough fleas – but since she didn't understand cat language, how could they tell her that?

12

Felina carefully put her paw through the cage and tapped the recipe, which Scarlett still held in her hand. Felina kept tapping until Scarlett said, 'What? You want it back?' and pushed it out of the cage on to the floor.

Felina arranged the recipe on the ground in front of her and studied it carefully. Felina could read human writing, but only very slowly. She was looking for the word 'flea'. She knew it was a short word that began with the human letter 'f' and after she had paused briefly at the words 'fur' and 'full', she finally found the word 'fleas' and placed her paw under it. Then she looked at Scarlett and miaowed urgently at her.

Scarlett looked at the spot where Felina had placed her paw. '*No fleas . . .*' she read

204

out, but she still didn't seem to get the message.

'Start scratching, everybody,' Felina urged the others. 'That ought to make her understand.'

So they all sat down and started to scratch themselves as energetically as they could.

'I *have* got a flea-comb in my pocket,' Scarlett said slowly as it dawned on her what the cats were asking her to do. 'Aunt Bunty asked me to use it on Mephisto this morning, after I'd taken India to the vet. So are you saying that if we put some fleas into the hairballs it might stop this anti-tagging spell from working?'

'Yes!' the cats miaowed together.

'I can't imagine why Bunty thought *I* might have fleas,' Mephisto murmured, 'but it's just as well you brought a flea-comb with

you under the circumstances, I suppose.
Now . . . who wants to go first?'

'I'm sure *I* can donate quite a few,' Albert-
of-the-street miaowed cheerfully, as he
climbed on to Scarlett's lap to let her begin.

'I'll need to put the fleas straight into the
hairballs after I catch them,' Scarlett said.
'Otherwise they'll jump away and we'll lose
them.'

So the cats began to transport the hairballs from the table to Scarlett, who was able to reach out through the bars of the cage and pick them up. Mia then made a hole in each one with her claw, ready for Scarlett to drop in a flea.

By the time Scarlett had finished combing Albert-of-the-street, they had placed fleas inside a total of twenty-eight hairballs. All the cats thanked him very enthusiastically, since none of them could imagine being able to donate even half that number themselves.

It was Mia's turn next, and Felina was surprised when Scarlett found eight fleas on her.

'I expect it's because you've been mixing a lot with certain other cats lately,' Mia's mother mewed, glancing rather pointedly in Mephisto's direction.

207

Cosmo offered to go next, standing up against the bars of the cage so that Scarlett could put her hand through and comb him. Cosmo had fourteen fleas, which was more than he'd expected, and he felt quite proud of his contribution.

Tani volunteered to go next, but Scarlett couldn't find a single flea on her. 'It's my Siamese fur,' Tani explained apologetically. 'Fleas don't seem to like it very much. I think it's too soft and fine for them.'

'I don't believe fleas like *my* coat very much either,' Felina said, moving forward to be combed. She was therefore extremely surprised when Scarlett found nine fleas on her.

'You probably caught them from me, Mother,' Mia said quickly.

'And you probably caught *yours* from *me*,' Cosmo told his friend.

Felina blinked her large amber eyes at

208

Mephisto. 'And I think we can guess who you caught *yours* from, Cosmo.'

Scarlett had been counting up the total number of fleas as she went along. 'We've found fifty-nine so far. That means we need another forty-one.'

'We only need forty really, because there's one hairball missing,' Cosmo pointed out.

Mephisto was the last to come under Scarlett's flea-comb, and all the cats watched as Scarlett ran the comb through his thick black coat and found that it was coming back with several fleas stuck between its prongs each time.

She collected the forty they needed quite easily. 'When we get out of here, I'll remove the rest,' she promised him.

Mephisto, who was feeling a lot less itchy all of a sudden, mewed to the others, 'I have

209

obviously been mixing a great deal too much with that Cleo Cattrap.'

After Scarlett had finished using her flea-comb, the cats set to work putting the flea-filled hairballs back on the table – along with the recipe itself. As Tani nudged the last hairball back into place, they heard a noise coming from the chimney.

The cats ran off and hid just as Selina Slaughter landed on the cushion with a thud.

She seemed in a good mood as she picked herself up and walked over to the table. 'Still here, my dears?' she joked to her prisoners.

The two cats spat at her, which just made her laugh.

'What are you going to do with those?' Scarlett demanded, pointing at a bundle of envelopes that Selina was holding, which seemed to have names written on them in green ink.

Selina gave her a gappy grin. 'Shouldn't you be more concerned with what I am going to do with *you*, my dear?' she teased. 'Still . . . since you can't do anything to stop me, I'll tell you. I am going to fill up these envelopes with hairballs and send them off to my helpers who will distribute them to all the lucky witches my friend Sybil has selected to escape with her. You see, the prisoners are sent out in groups to do their community service – either out on the street or in flea clinics. My accomplices and I will dress up as old ladies, or as witches with flea-ridden cats, and secretly slip each witch a hairball. *I* have the pleasure of taking Sybil's to her at the clinic just around the corner, and she says that as I'm such a dear friend she'd be honoured if I'd spit on hers myself! Then, at four o'clock precisely, all the witch-prisoners will swallow their hairballs – at which point their saliva will react with the other ingredients and they will be *de-tagged*! And then they will escape! Sybil has promised to strangle whichever cat is with her at the time, which should be super fun!' She started to cackle loudly.

Scarlett gaped at her. 'You mean the anti-tagging spell is for *them*?'

'Of course!' Selina narrowed her eyes.

'How do *you* know the name of it? I haven't shown you the recipe!'

'It was just a guess,' Scarlett told her quickly. 'You know, it's a very good plot ... I mean, Wow! It really is! But you still won't get away with it. Even if all those witches *do* escape, they won't be allowed to get far. The good witches will go out looking for them and they'll all be caught in no time. And then *you'll* be arrested too!'

'Oh, but the good witches won't have time to look for us, I'm afraid,' Selina said smugly. 'You see, we've prepared a little distraction for them – something to keep them occupied while we make our escape. It involves a rather nasty airborne spell that attacks babies, especially those with clipped toenails. The good witches will be kept very busy trying to reverse that spell before it does permanent damage – and if you want to know

213

what sort of damage, then imagine having a baby brother who says *oink oink* and has a little pink curly tail!' Selina started to cackle even louder.

Scarlett felt furious – and she also felt scared. 'If you hurt Spike, Mum and Dad and Aunt Bunty will all come after you. They won't stop until they find you!'

'I *was* worried about that,' Selina agreed, pausing in mid-cackle to catch her breath. 'That's why I've decided to keep *you* as my hostage. I'll tell your parents that if they try and find me, their precious daughter will come to a *very* sticky end!'

'You're really *evil*!' Scarlett gasped.

'Thank you, my dear, but I'm afraid that flattery will get you nowhere,' Selina replied smoothly. 'Now . . . I really must stop all this idle chit-chat and get to work.'

She started to fill up the envelopes with

hairballs, muttering a few witchy words over each one before tapping it lightly with her wand to send it off up the chimney on its way to whichever of her witch cronies was expecting it. Finally she placed the last four hairballs into her own envelope and put it in her pocket along with her wand. Then she turned to face her prisoners.

'Now,' she told them, 'I need that final hairball.' She squatted down and peered inside the cage at her two cat captives. 'I suppose I shall have to take one of you with me to visit Sybil. Who wants to volunteer?'

When both cats shrank back, she laughed and pointed a long green fingernail at Mia. 'Actually I think I'd better take you, my dear. We haven't got much time and it will be much easier for Sybil to cut through *your* tender layers than that big fat tomcat's.'

Albert-of-the-street started to protest

215

indignantly that he *wasn't* fat, but he suddenly thought better of it and kept quiet.

Felina, however, could hold back no longer. Before Selina had the chance to go anywhere near her kitten she leaped forward and bit the witch as hard as she could on her ankle. Tani leaped out of the shadows and bit the other ankle, and Mephisto and Cosmo came out from their hiding places and jumped on to her shoulders where they sank *their* teeth in as well.

Selina howled and screamed and danced about the room, eventually kicking off Felina and Tani, and shaking off Cosmo. Mephisto held on for longer until she managed to grab hold of his tail and pull it so hard that he was forced to loosen his grip. As soon as she had freed herself she made for the chimney and shot up it as fast as she

could. Luckily, she was wearing her rocket-thruster shoes.

The cats were left trapped in the cellar below.

After she had reached the top, Selina called down to them angrily. 'I'll deal with you later!'

Then the cats heard the fireplace swinging back into place and she was gone.

'When her plan backfires and all her friends get turned into frogs she's going to be even more angry,' Scarlett said. 'We've got to get out of here before she comes back.'

'Maybe the other cats will have sent for help by now,' Felina said.

'Don't count on it,' Mephisto said gloomily. 'That traitor Cattrap has probably got them all involved in another one of his ridiculous competitions by this time. I expect they've forgotten all about us.'

'Cleo's not that bad, Father,' Cosmo said now. 'I don't think he meant us any harm. He just got fooled into helping Selina because she offered to give him something he really wanted.' And even though he had promised he'd keep it a secret, he decided to tell the others what Cleo had told him the previous night. Maybe then, if they ever got out of here, his father wouldn't be so hard on Cleo.

'I bet she wasn't planning on doing anything at all to alter his face,' Tani said after she had listened to the story.

'Or maybe she *was* . . .' said Felina, who had found another spell recipe lying on the edge of the table, and had been busy reading it while the other cats were talking. 'This is a spell to make a cat grow a long pointy nose.'

'Cleo asked for a shorter nose, not a longer one,' Cosmo said. 'Selina must be planning to trick him as well.'

'Serves him right, the fluffed-up fool,' Mephisto grunted.

Just then they heard a grating noise above them as if the fireplace was moving again. Then they heard a familiar miaow – a miaow that made Mephisto instantly start hissing – and they realized that Cleo himself was there.

Cleo tumbled down the chimney and Mephisto pounced on him immediately. 'Come to gloat, have you? Or were you expecting your friend Selina to be here waiting for you?'

But to their surprise, Cleo was closely

followed by Bunty, who landed with a thud on the cushion beside him.

'Aunt Bunty!' Scarlett cried out.

'What are *you* doing here, Scarlett?' Bunty gasped.

Scarlett quickly told her what had happened. 'But how did you know where to find me?'

'I didn't. I came here to look for the cats.' Apparently Cleo had got worried when the other cats hadn't returned to the school, and had gone to the Two-Shoes' house to see if they were there. That was how he had met Bunty, who was there looking for Scarlett. 'When Cleo told me what had happened I alerted the Good Witches' Society and came straight here,' Bunty explained.

'How did you find the hidden chimney?' Scarlett asked.

'I nearly didn't . . . until Cleo mentioned

that when he visited Selina for tea, the fireplace seemed to be moving as he was shown into the room. That was what made me think there might be a downwards chimney.' Bunty was kneeling down beside the cage door as she spoke, examining the padlock. Now she took her wand out of her pocket and tapped the padlock with the tip

of it, muttering the words of an unlocking spell at the same time. Immediately the end of her wand became key-shaped.

Bunty quickly unlocked the door and released Scarlett and the two cats.

'Aunt Bunty, we've found out why all the witch-babies' toenails were stolen,' Scarlett said. 'A hundred witches, including Sybil, are going to use the Broom sisters' anti-tagging spell to escape while they're doing their community service today. And Selina is planning to set loose another spell on all the babies afterwards. But don't worry, because we've already thought of a way to stop them!' Scarlett quickly showed her aunt the anti-tagging recipe, which Sybil had left lying on the table, and explained how they had added fleas to the spell in order to render it useless.

Bunty shook her head in amazement as

she heard about the Great Escape plan. 'I can't believe Sybil and Selina thought they could get away with this. Well it's too late to stop the witches leaving prison for the afternoon – they'll all have started their community service by now. But perhaps we'd better warn them that their escape plan is doomed and give them the chance to go back to prison rather than be turned into frogs.'

'*I* think we should let them be changed into frogs,' Mephisto said. 'Frogs don't taste very nice, but they make very good play-things – especially if they're good hoppers.'

'I'm not sure what the Good Witches' Society will say about that, Mephisto,' Bunty said, smiling. She quickly waved her wand and two pairs of rocket-thruster shoes appeared – one adult-sized and one child-sized. 'Scarlett and I will carry you all up the chimney and then we'd better go and tell the other good witches what's been happening. After that, I think a trip to Sybil's flea-clinic is in order. I don't suppose any of you wants to come with me and pose as my flea-ridden cat, do you?'

And every paw in the room shot up at once.

225

13

The flea-clinic where Sybil and four other prisoners were working as reluctant volunteers had five de-fleaing rooms and a waiting room. At the moment one customer in particular was spending a long time with Sybil. If anyone had looked in on them, they would have seen that the customer didn't even have a cat inside her basket, although she had pretended to talk to one while she was in the waiting room. ('Don't you worry, pusskins, we'll have those fleas removed in no time – there's no need to hide under that blanket!')

The customer was Selina Slaughter, and now that she was alone with Sybil she had dumped the basket on the floor. She was grinning as she carefully placed Sybil's hair-ball, which had the green toenails sticking

226

out of it and which Selina had just spat on, into a plastic bag before handing it to Sybil.

'The spell will work as soon as you and this hairball come into contact,' Selina told her friend. 'But wait until four o'clock before you actually touch it – then everyone will be escaping at the same time. I'll be waiting outside the window with your broomstick. I've just managed to slip hairballs to the witches in the next three rooms, but who-ever's in the room at the end will have to do without, I'm afraid. We're one hairball short.'

'Murdina Broom is in the end room,' Sybil said. 'She did promise to give me that special spell after we'd escaped – but never mind! I'm sure I can find another way of dis-posing of that pesky Cosmo.'

'I can try and make one of the other three witches give up *their* hairball if you like,' Selina suggested.

'Oh, don't trouble yourself. Murdina's been getting on my nerves in any case. She keeps boasting about how this Great Escape plan is really down to *her* brilliance rather than mine, because *she* provided the spell recipe. This will serve her right!'

Selina left Sybil with her hairball – now fully activated – and on her way out through the waiting room she didn't look at the other witches who were there. If she had done, she would have noticed Bunty and a smaller person who was hiding under a large red cloak. The two had just arrived and were sitting with a cat basket on the seat between them. Bunty had already spoken to the prison guard, who had now gone outside to make an urgent call on her mobile.

'The Good Witches' Society said they'd report the Great Escape plot to the prison governor,' Bunty said to Scarlett who had slipped off her cloak as soon as Selina had gone. 'But there probably won't be time for all the guards to be alerted.' She looked at her watch. 'It's nearly four o'clock now.'

'You mean the guards won't be able to stop the bad witches getting turned into frogs?' Scarlett said.

'If Sybil and her friends persist in trying to escape, there'll be nothing the guards can do about it,' Bunty replied.

'I don't want to miss seeing that!' Cosmo mewed enthusiastically from inside his basket.

'I suppose I should really go and warn Sybil while there's still time,' Bunty said. 'Scarlett, you'd better stay here. What takes place at four o'clock might not be a pretty sight. In fact, I'm not sure you should really witness it either, Cosmo.'

'*I'm* not squeamish,' Cosmo protested.

229

'Mia and *I dissected* a frog the other day, because Professor Felina wanted to show us how the inside bits of frogs are different from the inside bits of mice. We're doing toads next week.'

Bunty sighed. 'Sometimes I forget you're a cat, Cosmo. Why would you be squeamish? Come on then.' And she lifted up the cat basket and knocked on the door of Sybil's room.

'Come in! Come in!' Sybil called out in her best, fake-nice voice. When she saw who it was, she couldn't have been more delighted. 'Why, Bunty, my dear, what a surprise to see you again so soon. Have you brought that old witch-cat of yours . . . I forget his name . . . to be de-flead?'

'My witch-cat is not at all old,' Bunty said sharply, 'nor does he have fleas. This is one

230

of my sister's cats, who you already know very well.'

As Bunty opened the lid of the cat basket, Sybil shrieked with delight when she saw which cat it was. '*Cosmo!*' She had to struggle to keep her hands from slipping into a strangling grasp as she glanced at the clock, which said that it was two minutes to four. 'I find I work better if the little dears are left

alone with me,' she told Bunty slyly, as her hand felt about in her pocket to check that her hairball was still there.

'I don't think that's a very good idea, Sybil,' Bunty said. 'Anyway, we aren't here for your de-fleaing services. You see, we know all about your escape plan.'

At that moment the prison guard knocked on the door and came in. 'I've just spoken to the governor, Sybil. She says that if you're part of this Great Escape attempt, then you'd better forget it. The spell won't work. You've been found out.'

Bunty quickly asked the guard if she had told the other witches.

'Yes, but they think it's a bluff. They're all acting as cool as cucumbers, apart from Murdina Broom, who seems very agitated.'

'Of course it's a bluff!' snapped Sybil, who had now moved closer to the open window.

'Somehow you've got wind of our plan, but I'm afraid you're too late!' And she took the hairball from her pocket, tipped it out of its bag and cradled it in her palm, at which point it began to give off a faint greenish glow. Then, just for good measure, she popped it into her mouth and swallowed it.

Before the others could stop her, she jumped up on to a chair (that she had already placed under the window) and was about to leap outside, when the electronic tag attached to her ear started to beep loudly. There was just time for Sybil's face to contort into a furious scream before she turned green all over and green sparks started to shoot out of her body in all directions. Then her scream turned into a croak, and the next thing they saw was a large frog hopping right off the chair and out through the window.

Almost instantly they heard a disgusted shriek from outside. They rushed over to look and found Selina crouching underneath the window with a large croaking frog perched on her head. Still squealing, she reached up and swiped it on to the ground where it hopped away quickly into the bushes. Three other frogs could also be seen hopping away across the grass, and only Murdina Broom was left, her earring tag still in place, staring out of the window in total shock.

And so in one afternoon the local frog population was increased by nearly a hundred and, as the local cat population was to comment later, all the new frogs seemed to be exceptionally good hoppers.

The other cats were still waiting to hear what had happened, so Bunty dropped Cosmo back at his house before taking Scarlett up to the hospital to see her parents.

Cosmo climbed up on to the kitchen table and told his audience of Mephisto, Tani, Felina, Mia, Hagnus and Matty the whole story of how Sybil had been turned into a frog, and how Selina had been arrested immediately afterwards. Then he jumped down and went upstairs to repeat everything to India, who was lying down in the Moses basket in the bedroom.

'It sounds like you were very brave, Cosmo,' his mother told him. 'I'm very proud of you. But you also look like you could do with a good wash. Come here and let me lick you.'

235

'I think I'm old enough to lick *myself* clean from now on, Mother,' Cosmo said, staying where he was. 'Anyway, you're going to have plenty of other kittens to wash soon, aren't you?'

'*Very* soon, I think,' India agreed. 'Go and get your father, will you, Cosmo? Tell him I think it's nearly time.'

Cosmo hurried back downstairs to find that Mephisto, Felina and Tani were having a heated discussion about something, and that Mia, Matty and Hagnus were racing excitedly around the room.

Cosmo had to tap his father quite hard on the back to get his attention. 'Mother says she thinks it's nearly time,' he mewed urgently.

The adult cats instantly became quiet. 'I'd better go up and see if she needs anything, then I must come downstairs and wait,' Mephisto said, sounding very serious.

236

'I'll come upstairs with you,' Felina offered. 'She might need some help. Why don't you take the kittens to the competition, Tani? It will be probably be better if they're out of the way.'

'What competition?' Cosmo asked.

'Cleo is about to hold his catwalk final for the adult cats,' Tani told him. 'Meowface came to tell us about it while you were upstairs. He wanted to know if I was still going to take part.'

'You are, aren't you, Mother?' Hagnus called out.

'It does seem a shame to miss it,' Tani mewed.

So it was decided that Mephisto and Felina would stay with India, while Tani took the kittens with her to the school.

*

Cleo, Meowface and the adult finalists (including Albert-of-the-street) were already there when Tani and the kittens arrived. Cleo himself seemed deep in conversation with the female Persian, Tallulah Poppypuss, who had apparently been trying to comfort Cleo since he'd found out that Selina wouldn't be doing a nose-shortening spell on him after all.

'She's been telling him that having a perfect Persian face like hers, isn't as wonderful as he thinks,' Meowface said, 'because her humans are always taking her to *their* sort of cat shows, where she has to sit in a cage and get stared at all day. She's been trying to convince him that *he's* the lucky one, not her. And get this . . . She actually *licked* his nose a few minutes ago. I've never seen him let another cat lick his nose in all the time I've known him!'

As the catwalk final began, the kittens

238

watched from the side excitedly, and since there was only a small crowd this time they all cheered extra-loudly as each cat finalist walked very slinkily up and down the cat-walk bench.

After all ten cats had walked up and down twice, Cleo (who seemed rather pleased to be the only judge again) jumped up on to the bench himself and walked along it very nimbly before declaring that he was now going to announce the winners in reverse order. He waited for all the cheering and calling out of finalists' names to stop before shouting out, 'The runners-up are as follows . . . *third place* goes to our only alley-cat finalist! Will Albert-of-the-street please step forward to collect his prize?'

Everyone miaowed their congratulations as Albert-of-the-street bounded forward to take a bow and collect his fish fingers.

'*Second prize*,' Cleo continued, 'goes to our elegant Siamese finalist – Tani.'

Hagnus and Matty leaped about with excitement as Tani was awarded her prize of a meal for two at a local fish restaurant (and promptly went over to ask Albert-of-the-street if he happened to be doing anything that evening).

'Finally, I wish to announce the winner,' Cleo miaowed, pausing dramatically until the room was silent again. 'The winner of *Cleo Cattrap's Amazing Catwalk Extravaganza* is . . . the incredibly well-groomed . . . extra-ordinarily gracious . . . beauty of beauties . . . feline of felines . . .' And to everyone's amaze-ment he called out the name of Tallulah Poppypuss – who was now making enormous gooey eyes at him.

'But she's a *Persian*!' Meowface spluttered in total disbelief.

As all the other cats miaowed their applause, Cleo purred and rubbed his head against his new catwalk queen, who was doing the same back.

'Don't tell me he's fallen in love!' Meowface miaowed – so loudly that every cat in the assembly hall heard him and started to cheer even louder.

'It looks like it,' Cosmo said happily. And he suddenly got the feeling that from now on, Cleo wouldn't mind any more about not having a perfectly flat nose.

Cosmo and Mia arrived back at the house to find that the Two-Shoes family had come home from the hospital. Cosmo was delighted to see Scarlett, who was sitting in the kitchen with Spike on her lap while Goody made them all a pot of eye-of-newt tea.

241

'Do you know, now that we're home I suddenly feel completely worn out?' Gabriel called from the living room, where he had just finished brushing off the grey cat hairs from the seat of his favourite armchair.

Mephisto was curled up on the rug in front of the fireplace, looking worn out too.

'Father, have the kittens been born yet?' Cosmo asked him.

Mephisto opened one eye very slightly and murmured, 'Of course they have – why do you think I'm looking so exhausted?'

Cosmo and Mia raced upstairs to find that Felina was guarding the door of the bedroom. 'You can go in, Cosmo, but you must be very quiet,' she told him. 'No tearing about!'

Cosmo crept into the room and went over to the Moses basket, where India was lying on her side being suckled by her newborn kittens. Cosmo stood and stared at them. He couldn't believe how tiny they were – or how many of them there seemed to be!

'Felina was right about the heartbeats,' his mother said. 'There *were* nine – but one was mine, which means there are only eight kittens.'

'*Only* eight!' Cosmo repeated, staring in awe at his new brothers and sisters, and thinking that eight still seemed like an awful lot to him.

'Where's your father?' India asked.

'He's curled up on the rug downstairs,' Cosmo said. 'He says he's exhausted.'

'Is he *really*?' India sounded less than amused, but before she could say anything else, they heard footsteps on the stairs.

It was Scarlett. 'Now, Spike,' they heard her say, 'it's time for your nap. Come and see your lovely new Moses basket.'

The bedroom door opened and Scarlett walked in, carrying her baby brother in her arms. 'Wow!' she gasped when she saw India.

And India started to mew at her, most indignantly, that the extremely large-and-comfy cat basket was already too full and that she couldn't possibly make room for a witch-baby as well.

**'A-A-A-TISHOO!' Cosmo burst out, sending a huge
shower of magic sneeze into the cauldron.**

Cosmo has always wanted to be a witch-cat, just like his
father, so when he passes the special test he's really
excited. He can't wait to use his magic sneeze to help Sybil
the witch mix her spells.

Sybil is very scary, with her green belly button and toenails, and no one trusts her. So when she starts brewing a
secret spell recipe – and advertising for kittens – Cosmo
and his friend Scarlett begin to worry. Could Sybil be
cooking up a truly terrifying spell? And could the extra-
special ingredient be KITTENS?

A purrfectly funny and spooky story starring one brave
kitten who finds himself in a cauldron-full of trouble.

Do you believe in fairies?

When Rosie finds a tiny tartan sock in her bedroom she's sure it could only fit one thing – a fairy! Mum tells Rosie not to be so silly: fairies don't exist.

Then the old lady who lives next door tells Rosie that Mum's the one who's silly – fairies are everywhere if you know how to look. And they love chocolate.

Rosie's not sure who to believe until she sees something in the grass at the top of the moor and then she can hardly believe her eyes. It's fluttering and tiny and magical. Could it really be a fairy . . . ?

A selected list of titles available from Macmillan Children's Books

The prices shown below are correct at the time of going to press. However, Macmillan Publishers reserves the right to show new retail prices on covers, which may differ from those previously advertised.

Gwyneth Rees

Mermaid Magic (3 books in 1)	ISBN-13: 978-0-330-42632-9 ISBN-10: 0-330-42632-X	£4.99
Fairy Dust	ISBN-13: 978-0-330-41554-5 ISBN-10: 0-330-41554-9	£4.99
Fairy Treasure	ISBN-13: 978-0-330-43730-7 ISBN-10: 0-330-43730-5	£4.99
Fairy Dreams	ISBN-13: 978-0-330-43476-8 ISBN-10: 0-330-43476-4	£4.99
Fairy Gold	ISBN-13: 978-0-330-43938-1 ISBN-10: 0-330-43938-3	£4.99
Cosmo and the Magic Sneeze	ISBN-13: 978-0-330-43729-5 ISBN-10: 0-330-43729-1	£4.99

For older readers

The Mum Hunt	ISBN-13: 978-0-330-41012-0 ISBN-10: 0-330-41012-1	£4.99

All Pan Macmillan titles can be ordered from our website, www.panmacmillan.com, or from your local bookshop and are also available by post from:

Bookpost, PO Box 29, Douglas, Isle of Man IM99 1BQ
Credit cards accepted. For details:
Telephone: 01624 677237
Fax: 01624 670923
Email: bookshop@enterprise.net
www.bookpost.co.uk

Free postage and packing in the United Kingdom